THRUM

A Conspiracy to Create Euphoria

Pete Lans

THRUM
PETE LANS

Author: Lans, Pete
Title: Thrum
Edition: 2nd ed.
ISBN: 978-0-6483227-0-2

Originally published in 2014

Cover design and illustrations
Nadia Asserzon and Rebecca Timmis 2014

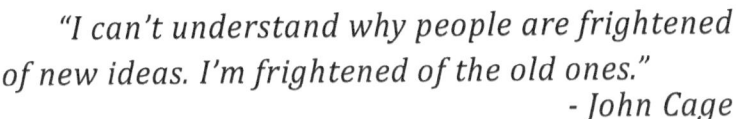

"I can't understand why people are frightened of new ideas. I'm frightened of the old ones."
- John Cage

"One woman I know said it was the funniest book she'd ever read."
- Thrum Reviewer

More Books by Pete Lans

The Difference

Realm of the Conspirators

About the Author

Pete Lans is in his sixties now and has at last decided on a career: being a writer. After a lifetime of optimistic inventing and building, all without a hint of commercial gain, his two daughters have advised him to stick to what he's good at: telling stories.

He lives in Brisbane, Australia, but is considering joining the endless migration of nomads traversing the country in search of free camping and friendship.

Or, if the opportunity presents itself, he would like to develop the Roadworks Learning concept mentioned in his novel, *Realm of the Conspirators*, and do his bit to transform the lives of children and to help them escape the programmed future for which they are presently destined.

A Tranquil Void

When I think back to how it all began, it's hard to believe; and yet, so many people have asked me to tell the story. 'You write it, Ian. You know what happened. Why don't you write it?' was what I often heard. So, I sat down, with a heart full of memories, and recorded the events that I had set in motion not so long ago.

All of us lived in Butcherville at the time—a ghastly name for an ordinary country town. It's how the name got changed that the story is about—the things that happened that led us one day to congregate near the new sign at the bridge and acknowledge the change in our destiny.

I was born here, as were many of the others, and a few of us were at school together. I don't remember that much about the people around me—I'm an inventor and I've always tended to live in my ideas. I regret that now. Some people have such a strong ability to engage in the gritty present; life for them is so consequential. That is why I'm writing this; because my friends struggled with meaningful lives while I blithely dealt with good fortune. I'm doing my best to atone for being someone who didn't

1

always recognise the ebb and flow of need in those around me.

This is a pretty part of the world. Worn out and over-cleared generations ago, there's a softness returning to the line of the hills and the wend of the creeks. Young people can't wait to leave the area, but it's surprising how many return—usually to take over the family farm. The mail train still runs through here, but it doesn't carry any mail, and the highway bypasses the town now by many miles. I sometimes think the tranquillity can become oppressive, but then we have a flood, or bushfires, and the community rallies and we forget about our insignificance and try to achieve the impossible.

Sonya and I live in a large old Queenslander on a leafy corner block. We bought it when some engineering work that I did for the railways paid out rather well. That was over thirty years ago and the children have come and gone. It all happened so quickly. If I could do it all again, I would hold every dirty nappy and every waking cry dear to my heart. Of course, the family thinks I'm becoming old and sentimental; they assure me that I can hold all the dirty nappies and hush all the fretful cries I want to when the grandchildren arrive.

Sonya saves me from myself almost daily; any material gain that we've acquired over the years is due to her good sense.

I'm semi-retired now. I do consultation work all around the country, but a lot of the time I'm at home, mostly toying with some gadget or another in the old shed.

That's where the story begins—in the old shed, and for once, I know more about things than anyone else.

Pretty Neighbour

In a sunny garden, at the end of a rambling, trellised passionfruit vine, the forces of nature are at work, changing the mind of men—and women. Just like the ants crawling over the flowers, minute and irresistible, the cosmic forces tease and provoke the consciousness of Ian Shaw as he tinkers in the solitude of his shed, building a device for which he can think of no practical application. A passionfruit flower, white with a vivid yellow and purple centre, brushes against the pane of the small window. Inside, an old transistor radio on the workbench emits the tinny sound of *The Ink Spots* singing *Until the Real Thing Comes Along*.

Seated on a chair at his workbench, Ian applies a soldering iron to a circuit board. A slow curl of smoke rises above his steady hand. A little unkempt, but with a pleasant face, he is peering through a large magnifying glass on a stand, and frowning with concentration. The desk lamp is the only light source. The whorl of smoke rises upwards to the shadows amongst the trusses and drifts between the strange constructions of metal and wood lodged amongst the beams. The dusty tangle of past projects continues right up to the corrugated metal roof.

A sudden thump emanates from above, followed by soft scratching.

Ian takes his eyes away from the magnifying glass and squints up into the gloom. He waits briefly, then turns and lowers his hand back to the circuit board. Another plume of smoke rises lazily from the bench. With a pair of tweezers, Ian holds down the board as he blows over its surface with a little puffer.

Again, there comes a scuttling and scraping sound. Ian puts down the things in his hands, reaches over to the radio and turns down the volume. His frown deepens as he listens. A thin screech issues from beyond the nestled junk above him. Pushing back his chair, he gets up and walks amongst the clutter to the back door.

When he opens it, the light is bright and harsh. He steps outside and walks around to the corner of the shed near the high paling fence. Shielding his eyes from the glare, Ian looks up to the roof.

His neighbour, Tiffany, is straddling the space between the shed and the fence, one knee hitched up over the gutter and one stretched foot on the fence rail. About thirty, and lovely to look at, she is reaching out to retrieve a Frisbee and is rather disadvantageously exposed to Ian's sight.

With her chin pressed against the corrugations, she looks down at him and says through squashed lips, 'When you've finished perving up my skirt, Ian, you

5

might think about getting me a ladder.'

With a mystified squint, Ian scrutinises Tiffany's silhouette. 'Oh, yeah,' he says, but remains staring with his head cranked. 'I won't be a moment.'

Without being able to move for fear of sliding, Tiffany tries to maintain her composure. She beseeches the heavens and shakes her head. She tries to relax as much as possible, gripping the warm metal even with her cheek in order to hold her position. A knowing smile forms on her distorted mouth. *We have been introduced... probably doesn't remember. Won't forget me now.*

With a disbelieving snort and a shake of his head, Ian re-enters the shed. 'Won't be a moment,' he says again, his voice trailing off.

After some time, and a lot of shuffling and grunting from below, the top of the ladder bangs against the gutter next to Tiffany's leg.

'You can come down now.'

Tiffany slides her foot to the nearest rung and, with a faint screech of fingernails on tin, she begins an awkward descent.

Clutching the ladder with both hands, Ian monitors Tiffany's progress with shifting eyes. Then, submitting to what is proper, he lowers his face as her skirt drapes over his bowed head.

Tiffany comes to rest on the lowest rung and turns to face him. She brushes away the material and drops in between his arms. 'Thank you, Ian.' She flicks the toy over the fence.

'Thanks, Mum!' cries a girl's voice from the other side. 'Thanks, Tiffany!' echoes another. Their laughter fades as they run off.

Tiffany rests her hands on her neighbour's shoulders. With the tiniest smirk on her face, she runs her eye over the wisps and strands of his still bowed head. 'Will you remember me for the rest of your life?'

Ian nods.

She smiles and draws herself to him in a little hug. 'Thanks again for saving me.'

'Do you want me to help you over the fence?' Ian motions with his head.

Tiffany purses her lips and raises a brow. 'No thanks, Ian. I'll go back through your garden—if that's okay?'

'Of course. Sorry.' He looks stricken. 'You'll have to go through the shed—the passionfruit has tangled up the gate. It won't open.'

Tiffany takes her hands from Ian's shoulders. 'Okay, then...'

He lets go of the ladder, as though sorry to end this small intimacy. With his head thrust downward, like a tracker searching the terrain, he leads the way to the shed door. He stands aside and drums his fingers on the frame as Tiffany enters. The two of them block much of the light from the doorway.

With small steps, Tiffany moves deeper into the dim disorder. 'Tell me that your mind isn't like this, Ian. It will make me feel a lot more comfortable.'

He fumbles for the light switch near the door. 'Huh? Oh, no—it doesn't work. The light. Sorry.' He brushes at his hair with his fingers. 'The roller door is straight through. Just mind the junk.'

Tiffany negotiates her way towards the roller door, now and then running her hand over various contraptions and devices. 'What do you do in here?' She pauses at the bench and surveys the objects lying under the lamp.

Ian shifts from standing to leaning and back again. 'Ah, I make things. Invent things.'

'Oh. You invent things.' Tiffany looks up into the trusses at the weird assemblage of objects lodged there. 'You solve problems. Is that what you do?' She turns with a dimpled smile.

'Sometimes. Quite frequently, mostly...' He tries to save himself. 'The roller door is straight ahead.'

Tiffany peruses the bench before pointing to the circuit board. 'What are you working on here?'

Ian moves forward with some hesitation. 'This?'

'Is it a radio?'

'Ah, no.'

'Hmmm? What then?'

Ian's gaze centres on the bench top. 'It's a... sonic... mixer...'

There is a longish moment of silence. Then, with a deft move, Tiffany reaches for the lamp and shines it into her rumpled neighbour's face. 'Tell me the truth—what does it do?'

Ian grimaces and averts his eyes. 'It mixes—without touching. Tiffany, I can't see.'

'Mixes what, Ian? Milkshakes? Poison? Magic? Is

8

it a super-hygienic smoothie machine?' She lowers the light. Her face resumes its playful contours. She brushes away an errant lock of hair.

The light seems to have awoken Ian. He blinks, raises his chin and gives Tiffany a rueful smile. 'Sorry. Um, it *is* Tiffany, isn't it?'

She dips her eyes.

'I'm in a strange... ah, just at the moment...' Ian scratches the back of his head. 'To be truthful, I have no idea what I've made here.' He reaches over and picks up a small metal box from the bench top. 'It's just an idea that I had—quite unbidden, and of no use at all as far as I can see.' He holds it out to her with an apologetic shrug. 'This is a prototype.'

On top of the box is a little conical spout and on the front is a control dial. Tiffany hefts the box in her hands. 'Does it do anything?'

'Well, there's nothing to see.' Ian takes it out of her hand and places it on the bench. He plugs in a power supply and rotates the dial. A soft hum emanates from the box. 'Put your palm about here,' he holds his hand a little way above the spout.

Tiffany moves closer to the bench and holds her hand over the box. She withdraws it with haste. A look of shock and disgust transforms her face. 'Oh! It's touching me!'

Ian looks apologetic. 'That's what it does.'

Tiffany returns her hand above the projecting spout. She experiments with different distances. 'It's pulsing. It feels like it's touching me—but it's not.' She shakes her head in wonderment. 'That's weird, Ian.'

He smiles broadly and holds Tiffany's eye with an easy confidence.

A New Start

Tiffany stops at the bottom of the front stairs to her house and looks across at her neighbour. Ian closes the roller door which squeals and squeaks all the way to the floor. She holds the handrail and thinks about the life that had closed for her—the reason why she needed to start again, alone, with Jane. She steps up to the veranda and lets herself into the old house. The hallway is dark and cold and she moves quickly towards the sunroom at the back of the house. The windows are open. She looks at the big mango tree outside and wonders why she chose to move north.

Living here was a comfortable respite from the clamour of the city, but as yet, Tiffany had not discovered a place for her soul; it was the momentum of routine that pushed her onward. She was waiting for the complement to her life—something she thought she had, but that had been taken away so emphatically.

She lowers herself onto the armrest of a heavily upholstered armchair and topples backwards onto the seat.

It was the sneaking complacency that had done

it—destroying a marriage as effortlessly as jealousy, or an affair, or money troubles. They had everything, and then, one day, they both realised that they needed to start again—before it was too late; they were each searching for different things.

Tiffany imagined that she needed to be... oh, a waitress—in a truckies' diner, paying rent, with the barest of furniture and having to help Jane adjust to a new life.

There was no acrimony, but there was no easy solution either. She cried in despair and desolation, not so much for Jane—her father's work enabled him to share a lot of time with her in exciting and exotic places—but because of her frustration at having such an incompatible sense of destiny.

And then, when she was alone on the train—the old mail train, spending long periods in sidings to let the coal trains past—she discovered a town that seemed to evoke a forgotten glory, and she wondered if she might find a trace of it to follow for herself.

But she didn't—not straight away.

One overcast day, she encountered Angela on her way to the roadhouse on the edge of town, who gave a chewing-gum grin when Tiffany asked her whether there was any work going. Tiffany thought that Angela was thoroughly engaged in a journey of the soul.

Angela thought that it was an amazing stroke of luck that she had found someone as decent as this who wanted to work in a diner.

Tiffany loved the work. It was either exhaustingly

hot in summer or freezing cold in winter; it was either hypnotically quiet or impossibly busy. The work was routine and uncomplicated, but Miranda, the owner, was never satisfied. She would bawl at the waitresses from within the kitchen and hurl her vexation at customers with no provocation at all.

And each afternoon, Tiffany would ride her bicycle home and make dinner and tell Jane about all the funny things that happened at work. Sometimes Jane would illustrate an incident with her colour pencils. The drawing would stay taped to the fridge for weeks.

Tiffany missed being in love; she liked the cluttered household that came with love. That was why the rooms were so spare; she refused to delude herself into thinking that life could be made full with material things. One day her home would be full of the things from a shared love.

Later that evening, she takes the single teacup from the drying rack, plucks the only teaspoon from the tray and, with an efficiency that bespeaks aloneness, makes herself a cup of tea. Then, she walks into the half dark sunroom and settles crosswise into the old armchair.

Tiffany's thoughts dwell on her encounter with her eccentric neighbour and the strange machine that he is making. Her fingers twitch on her teacup when she recalls the machine's invisible touch. It was as though it was a solid, pulsing hologram.

She swigs back her tea and puts the cup on the ground. A lusty sexuality asserts itself. With the tiniest smile, she shapes her body to the chair and throws a leg over the backrest. Her fingers slide down her belly, under her panties, and she touches herself sensuously. A moody redolence melds with the events of the day—a machine with the downy touch of a feather and the fortitude of a fist.

Tiffany sits upright and peers across the room through the windows of the sunroom. There is enough light outside to make out the silhouette of the house next door. A dim yellow glow comes from the kitchen window. She swings her legs to the ground and walks over to the phone.

Good Neighbours

Ian and Sonya are seated side by side, each in a comfortable armchair. A small telephone table is nestled between them. They face the television in the lounge room, but it is not on. They are both reading, and Sonya is knitting as well. She is pleasantly plump with an attractive, natural smile. Attached to her reading glasses is a tiny laser transmitter. To the other side of Sonya's chair there is a pedestal with a mechanical arm that reaches over and holds her book for her. As Sonya reads, she clicks and clacks her needles with a languid rhythm. A bright little light begins to flicker on the end of one of the needles and Sonya casts to the next row without looking down. She reaches the end of the page and gives a small nod of her head. A fine metal tongue rotates at the bottom of the book holder and flips over to the next page.

'Cuppa tea, dear?' Ian says, still reading.

Sonya smiles.

The telephone rings softly between them. Ian, immersed in his book, reaches over and fumbles for the handset. He passes it across.

Sonya puts down her knitting and takes the phone.

'Hello, Sonya speaking,' she says in a voice that is vital and friendly, 'Oh, hello, Tiffany.' As she talks, the movement of her head causes the book holder to flip pages repeatedly. '… did he—on the roof! Whatever were you doing up there? Oh. Yes, he's right here. I'll put him on. Good night, Tiffany. Goodnight.'

At the mention of Tiffany's name, Ian stops fiddling with his ear and looks up from his book.

'Ian—it's Tiffany—you know, the new girl next door. She'd like a word with you.'

Ian extends his hand for the phone. His voice falters with surprise. 'Um, hello,' he leans forward, pressing at his brow with his other hand, '… oh, that's alright—it was no trouble at all. I quite—in fact, I… it was no trouble at all…'

Sonya readjusts the mechanical page turner and listens with a bemused curl to her lip.

'An idea! For my invention?' Ian squeezes the handpiece to his ear, '… right. Yes. Oh, I suppose not—couldn't do any harm. Now? Right now? Ah, oh, right-oh then. No, I don't mind. Yes, I'll see you at the roller door. Okay then. Goodnight, Tiffany. Goodnight.' He replaces the phone and engages his mind to the immediate task ahead. 'That was Tiffany,' he says, loudly enough to ripple the cosy domesticity.

'I know that, dear. What did she need to speak to you about?'

'She was stuck on the roof.'

'Really. But she *has* managed to get to a phone?'

'Oh, I helped her down this afternoon. She wants

to borrow my... you know, that sonic... apparently she thinks she might have a purpose for it.'

'You've been showing her around your shed, have you, Ian?'

'Yes. No, not really. She had to come through the shed because of the passionfruit... I showed her where the roller door...'

'And what has she got in mind for your invention?'

Ian looks quizzical. 'Don't know. She didn't say.'

He slides his book into position, but Sonya can see from the reflection in the television that he is not reading.

'And, you're meeting her at the shed? Ian?'

'Ah, yes. Yes. I'm going to give it to her in the shed.'

'Are you... well, just make it a quickie then, because you promised me a cup of tea, remember?'

Ian propels himself out of the chair. 'I'll put on the billy.'

Totally Unexpected

The next morning, Ian is seated at his workbench in the shed. The soldering iron is smoking in its holder nearby. He stares at the little square window, lost in thought.

The passionfruit flower has opened, and myriad insects crawl about its vital midst. It is the creative expression, not just of the plant, but of the entire realm of the organic cycle. The collective energy of hundreds of ants and bees is focused here, each creature taking something of the blossom's essence to germinate growth elsewhere. So, it is with Ian's idea—a flowering of the mind. His unique synthesis of technology will fertilise the sphere of existence that he shares with so many others.

He looks across at the empty space that the sonic prototype had occupied the day before. He looks at his watch, takes a deep breath and rubs his eyes.

His work has always been of a practical nature; engineers solve problems; they never intentionally create them. And there is the paradox—the more that gets invented, the more problems are created. There are precious few inventions that have actually contributed to better understanding between people; the toothbrush, maybe.

Ian is about to resume work when he hears something. He swivels around in his seat and faces the direction of Tiffany's house. He listens intently, then, with a tiny shrug, he reaches across for the soldering iron. Then he hears it again. He stands from his chair and walks to the roller door. Keeping his ear cocked, he bends and rolls up the noisy door. The bright morning light streams onto his face. He scans the street then looks across to the yard next door. The lawn and a few neglected shrubs glisten with the last of the dew. Taking a step out, he pauses with a finger to his mouth. Then, with his eye on the bottom tread of the stairs, Ian walks with slow steps towards the veranda of Tiffany's house.

Making house calls to women he barely knows, regarding an invention about which he is confused, is not something he can do with panache. But, when he has negotiated every step of the stairs and is standing with a bowed head at the front door, he hears something that makes him transgress even his strict bounds of decency, and he enters the house without knocking.

The screen door closes with a soft squeal. The hallway is long and dark. Ian is uneasy and full of doubt as he creeps along towards the sounds. He pauses with his hand around the corner at the end of the hall. He leans out and peers across the dining room to the sunroom beyond.

From across the room, Tiffany's anxious face stares at him over the back of the heavy armchair. Her brow is warped, and her mouth is open, but now silent. She is seated facing rearward, with her bare legs astride the bulging armrests and with her forearms and chin on the top of the backrest. There is an urgency in her face that repels Ian at first, but in a sudden collapse of mind that almost causes him to faint, he comes to the only, unimaginable, deduction. With his eyes locked on hers, he approaches with slow steps. When he is near, he rests his hand on Tiffany's shoulder. He can feel the sporadic tremors of her body.

Ian raises his sight to the windows and the mango tree outside. He recalls when he was a kid, getting stung by wasps when he was stealing mangoes, and how Mrs Stack had retrieved him and put a "blue bag" on his arm. Now, it is his turn to come to the rescue— of someone in the thrall of an orgasm. He has always been conscious of the vastness of the human theatre over time, but this occasion, he thinks, would have to be a first.

Ian feels something at his wrist and looks down to see Tiffany's fingers reaching out for him. He enfolds her hand in his. A distant humming comes to his attention. It seems to be emanating from under her gathered skirt. His gaze travels across the tanned skin of her leg. He spies Tiffany's knickers draped over the armrest. Leaning forward, he lowers himself over her body. The smell of her warm hair floats to his nostrils. With his free hand, he reaches behind her and carefully lifts Tiffany's skirt. Holding the folds of material against the small of her back with his forearm, he searches the seat cushion with his hand.

The humming becomes hypnotic; the moment is overwhelming. Tiffany's presence dominates his consciousness; she has become huge. There is so much to love about her. Beyond her helplessness, Ian recognises the powerful feminine counterpart to his masculinity, and, for the first time, he knows that there is a Goddess.

His fingers connect with cool metal. He opens his eyes that he hadn't been aware of closing. With his cheek pressed to Tiffany's temple, he grasps the sonic machine and slides it from beneath her.

Tiffany moans and slumps in the chair.

Lifting the device to his chest, Ian straightens and takes a few deep breaths. Then he bends and kisses Tiffany's hand, still limply clutching his own.

Indelicate Proposal

That afternoon, in the shed, Ian is unsure whether he should be thinking about the morning's events. It's not because of a moral discipline thing, but rather because Tiffany is seated across from him on the other side of the workbench and is obviously intent on discussing the incident in one way or another. He bends to his work and puffs non-existent dust from a circuit board. Should he even be working on this contraption any longer? At this moment, he could easily lose himself in his task, but that would be rude. He knows that he doesn't understand much about what happened, but he doesn't want Tiffany to agonise over it. He'll happily let things be; it's what he has always done, and things have worked out okay in the past.

A glance over the top of the magnifying lens reveals that Tiffany, contrite and motionless, is still sitting on the stool that he had provided for her. By now, the silence has gone on long enough for Ian to feel that the issue at hand is beginning to heal itself—or resolve itself, or whatever. Anyway, what does it matter that she, Tiffany, his new neighbour, had been using his gadget as… okay, that was unexpected. In fact, did women in general have such strong, sexual… Sonya?…

'I don't want to force you into discussing my behaviour, Ian,' Tiffany's soft voice fills the silence. 'I just want to tell you that I didn't mean for you to be upset… or embarrassed.'

'Oh, no,' Ian replies too quickly, 'I won't be embarrassed—I'm not embarrassed. And I won't discuss it with you. I mean, I will discuss it with you—if you want me to—if you want to—if I want to…'

Tiffany hooks her heels into the stool brace and jams her hands into her lap. 'Actually, I do want to discuss this with you.'

'Oh, you do.'

'Yes. Ian… I want you to make me one of those gadgets.'

He gives an incredulous smile. 'One of these? Whatever for?'

Tiffany's eyes roll with a hint of exasperation.

Ian looks appalled. 'Oh, right! Um, yeah. No trouble at all,' he nods gravely. 'To use… as…' He stills, stares and steeples his fingers.

Tiffany sighs. She grips and scrunches at the hem of her skirt. 'Look, Ian, if you're not comfortable with… doing this, then…'

Ian is nodding to himself with a faraway look on his face. 'Well, that's just the thing, isn't it—you've got to be comfortable.' He regards his neighbour with beatific calm.

Tiffany gives a resigned sigh. 'Yes,' she says.

'Exactly!' Ian pushes away from the bench and looks heavenward. 'I... ah, well, I'm not completely sure what a woman's needs are in this respect, but I would imagine that an easychair would be the most comfortable way of... um... to have... for the machine. Ah, a chair—don't you think?'

Tiffany bolts off the stool and stands with her hands clasped in front of the workbench. 'Oh, Ian—that's brilliant! An easychair would be ideal.'

'Yes, I thought so.' Ian stands and strokes his chin, resolutely engaged in the delight of a new project. 'Of course, you'd need a certain amount of adjustment in order to aim... um... for you to position... ah...'

Tiffany scrambles around the table and hugs him. 'You're a genius, Ian.'

Greater Forces

Tiffany looks back from the stairs of her house to the little weatherboard shed with the passionfruit vine growing against it. She can see the movement of Ian's legs as he struggles to close the stubborn roller door. This is what she has been waiting for; the moment when everything about her being begins to make sense; when everything that she is, and everything that she imagines she is, becomes like a little crystal seed, with perfect design and perfect inevitability.

The sunlight warms her bare arms. She looks at her hand, lightly gripping the rail. Her tanned skin seems remote, as though it is not her hand—not her arm—not her body that carries her burdens and toils through the day. She makes her legs climb the stairs and aims herself at the cane lounge sitting in the shade of the veranda. She settles into it and lets her head arch back against the wall. The shade is a relief. Gradually she reattaches herself to her body.

A thought begins to shape; she realises that, whilst she has ownership of her body, she must use it for a purpose; she is obliged to deliver herself to achieve something great. For a moment it all makes sense, but a falling palm frond breaks the spell. Tiffany blinks herself into the moment and walks inside, trying to reassemble the message.

That evening, Ian puts down the big coffee table book on archaeology and pauses, sitting forward on his chair with his fingers steepled. He applies his focus to a question—which should be innocuous enough—but one can never be sure—it's best to have a few answer options at hand. But no, it's simple enough! He's not being disingenuous. He is trying to avoid any unnecessary awkwardness—unnecessary suspicion. Suspicion! What is there to suspect?

'What are you going to ask me, dear?' Sonya's needles clack as she casts to a new row.

Ian leans back in his chair and touches his forehead in a feigned gesture of forgetfulness. 'I just... do we still need that old easychair in the sleep-out?'

'Oh, I suppose not,' Sonya says. 'Why?' She scratches her foot with her knitting needles.

Ian leans forward and hefts the book into his lap. 'Oh, Tiffany—you know, the new lass next door—she wants to buy a new chair for her... ah, sunroom.'

'Oh well, she can have it, Ian, if she wants it.'

Ian laboriously turns a page. 'Hmmm... I'll let her know.'

Sonya looks up over her book and purses her lips. 'She hadn't mentioned it to me when I looked after Jane the other night. She's been next door over a year now, you know.'

'A year!' Ian nods deeply into his book, 'Isn't that…' He looks up. In front of him, on the cabinet against the wall, are framed photographs of the family: on holidays when the children were young, graduations, engaged in sport, funny faces. On the dining table is a sewing machine, and draped over a chair back are Ian's overalls with neatly sewn patches on the elbows.

He feels oddly disassociated; did he really wear out the material so much that it became a hole? It's almost as though he is as much a piece of machinery as the ones he uses every day. 'Cuppa, dear?' he says, to restore his frame of mind.

Sonya smiles. She watches from the periphery of her vision as Ian rises from his chair, making the customary slap of the knee that once, a long time ago, was a vaguely humorous gesture meant to suggest capitulation on his part with regard to the roles that they were establishing in their relationship.

The needles cease their clicks and clacks. Sonya lays the length of knitting in her lap. With unfocused eyes, she views this episode of her life—a period of expectation. The passage of time has distilled a livelihood to which she has become irrevocably bound, and the search for identity has too often been subverted by her duties.

Recently, she'd become aware of a hollow anticipation, reproving herself for becoming dependent on the promise of grandchildren. It was a lovely thought, but she was ready to do more than be a doting grandmother. And, whatever she did, she would be doing it with the man she'd been with for all of her adult life. Would he be able to recognise her needs? Would he be able to change? Would she be able to love him if he couldn't? In many ways, she was in the prime of her life; now was her time to develop the natural attributes that had been enriched through a life dedicated to marriage and motherhood.

A Rare Gift

The passionfruit vine is compelled to bear fruit. That is the genius of nature; once the seed is sown, fruition is inevitable. Through the little square window of the shed, the hard, green skin of a baby passionfruit reflects the morning sunlight.

Inside, a space has been made for the newly modified easychair. It is a Scandinavian design of moulded plywood with thin padding and leather upholstery. It's very low, with armrests that can be raised in line with the backrest. A narrow slot along the centreline of the seat is trimmed with cloth tape. Inside the slot is the sonic pulse device—the improved model with a hand-held control box.

The seat is of generous width, and standing astride it, Tiffany holds her bunched skirt in front of her, with her scrunched panties spilling out of her hand. She lifts the bundle of skirt to her navel and looks down at the slot, at the aperture of the sonic beam. Her face reveals nothing as she lowers herself to meet the seat with her bare groin. Then, she stretches her legs onto the fold-out footrest, leans back and closes her eyes.

It had been surprisingly easy for her to duck under the half open roller door and meet Ian. She felt impelled, unashamed and eager. 'I'd better close the door then, shall I?' she'd said. But, Ian had jumped to the door and bent and wrestled with it until the shed became suddenly dark. He stepped over to the desk and switched on the table lamp. When he turned around, Tiffany was just stepping out of her panties. With a coy smile, she turned and moved next to the seat. 'I'm grateful to you, Ian...' and, whilst she wanted to say more, she didn't, but stepped astride the seat and looked down at the slot. What she had been thinking of had to do with a married man, his wife, a titillator device, a shameless neighbour and a small town—but she just couldn't compose anything coherent. In the end, she'd decided to be spontaneous and hope for an uncomplicated result.

Ian has been tightly gripping the control box for some time now and his fingers have begun a slight tremor.

He had intended to display a detached interest in the trialling of the chair, but no matter how he imagined the course of events playing out, he was unable to position himself in a dignified and authoritative role. In the end, lying awake next to Sonya the night before, he had decided to simply abandon any pretence and to just allow destiny, in the shape of his lovely neighbour, to take its course.

That is why he is looking lost and inert, standing at the foot of the chair, staring at Tiffany's bare feet.

Amongst the bizarre shapes and shadows in the shed, the two of them look oddly vulnerable to be pioneers.

Ian shifts his eyes to meet Tiffany's.

Through lowered lids she peers at him from the low-slung seat. She splays her knees so that the sides of her thighs rest comfortably on the leather seat. With slender fingers, she lowers the armrests and allows herself to relax.

Without taking his eyes from her, Ian rotates the dial one tiny fraction. He feels his legs going weak and plunges to his knees. With his head bent over the controller in his hands, he ever-so-slowly increases the increments on the dial and breathlessly listens for any sounds from Tiffany.

Tiffany looks about, focusing in and out at the eerie shadows cast in the trusses above her. She wriggles herself into a better position on the seat. There are feelings now that are sculpted and shaped; solid sounds, strummed and vibrant; she feels transported by a drumming that sweeps over endless expanses and plunges into fathomless voids. Her body fills with the ardour of an ancient blessing, and she inhales with a shudder.

Ian is left beholding a mystery that men have never divined and that women have mostly taken for granted. He reaches out and places the controller in her lap. Then he positions Tiffany's hand with her fingers pinching the dial. Slowly, he lowers his forehead to rest on her knee.

31

Intersections

On the outskirts of town, a semi-trailer rolls away from the bowsers and heads away on the country road. The roadhouse, where Tiffany works, is a sad nexus where people continually meet in incompatible circumstances.

One of these is Miranda, whose hostility has been honed by the delusion that she is a sexual extrovert. No one knows the truth about her; even she doesn't know why, at forty, she has become a caricature of the type of person she loathes. She dresses provocatively and is defiant to just about everyone. Miranda fully subscribes to the adage that the best defence is offence, and all the time that she is jousting with the truck drivers, she just can't work out why she hates it.

She wheels around the tables with plates balanced in her hands, revealing her ample bosom when she stoops to slide the meals unceremoniously to three drivers.

One of the drivers slyly studies Miranda's cleavage and, with a wink to his mates, murmurs, 'When are we gonna see the *full* menu, Miranda?'

'The full menu?' she answers malevolently, 'would be more of the same.' She pushes forward her breasts and stares him down. 'It's the *routine* that I love,' she groans, jerking backwards and forwards as though she is being regularly prodded from behind. 'It's sooo invigorating.' A lock of hair falls over her face and obscures half of her baleful stare. Miranda's face contorts into pained pleasure as she pulses in and out of the driver's face. Then, she rises from the table and plumps her hair. 'Oh... oh, that's better.' She gives a little shiver, smiles sweetly and turns away.

The driver blows through puffed cheeks and massages his brow. The others avoid his eye and pretend to find their food interesting.

Miranda strides back to the kitchen, past a table where a svelte young woman, nattily attired in a courier's uniform, is just taking a seat. On her shirt pocket is an embroidered bird in flight.

Miranda flicks a glance at the swift, flying across the arc of the woman's breast. She calls out behind her, 'One of the girls will be with you in a minute, love,' but stops in front of the swing doors. Her hand reaches down into the apron pocket to grasp the order pad. With her head lowered, she presses her fingers against her thighs and into the vee of her body. A hank of hair loosens itself and brushes her cheek. Miranda turns and looks—at the slender legs just crossing, and the elegant sandal dangling from a pointed foot. She walks back and flicks the hair from her face. 'What would you like... love?' she falters, meeting the woman's tiny smile.

'Yes, please,' she replies. Then, with a sudden, unguarded laugh, adds, 'I'm Siobhan.'

At the other end of the dining room, Angela looks across from where she is wiping a table and wonders why Miranda is taking an order when normally she is in the kitchen supervising the cooking and bawling out the staff. She reaches over the table and swings aside just in time to avoid a speculative embrace from one of the drivers. Angela is piqued—too riled to tick off the driver. She is preoccupied with thoughts about Tiffany. She glances over her shoulder. Behind her, Tiffany is taking an order from a group of road-train drivers. She has always been strangely naïve, but now she is pressing her skirt against the table edge as she scribbles in her pad. It's a breach of solidarity. All the girls know that, out here, *they* make the choices— especially pretty girls. And, out here there isn't much to choose from, so, all the girls feign boredom and cultivate a stratospheric superiority.

Except Claire, who, at seventeen, is intense and incompetent, and completely overwhelmed by the impasse in communication of everyone around her. She manages to drop an uneaten sausage onto the table as she is clearing. Only Tiffany had asked her about her music and the songs she wrote. One day Claire brought her guitar to work and played her newest song for Tiffany out in the car park. But Miranda had slammed open the screen door and called out that unless she was good enough to entertain in the dining room, she should get back inside.

Now, she moves to the table of road-train drivers and stands next to Tiffany, hoping to be as disarming.

Tiffany looks down with a little smirk. 'So, who's got the whopper?'

A beefy driver laughs and wraps his arm around Tiffany's waist. 'I've changed me mind,' he appeals to his mates, 'I'll have this dish instead.' He pulls her closer.

Everyone laughs, including Tiffany, who bows her head and plants a kiss on the man's huge forehead. 'Then I suppose you'll be wanting to *wash* the dishes as well, hey?'

There's more laughter and yahooing.

Tiffany rips out the order page and, with an affectionate pat on the driver's shoulder, she and Claire turn and head back to the kitchen.

Angela leans towards Tiffany as they collect cutlery behind the service screen. 'Tiff... are you expecting someone tonight?' she says with a demanding look, 'someone special, someone clean and charming—who doesn't read magazines with more meat in them than what's on his plate? Because it won't happen—you listening? So, wipe that look off your face and get real.'

Tiffany turns to her with a private smile and plonks a bunch of silver on Angela's tray.

Angela perseveres. 'What was that all about?' She nods in the direction of the dining room, 'So you're letting them paw you now? Mr Potato Head is going to be awfully fond of you, Tiffany, and next week you'll find yourself on his knee and his hand will be like a ferret on speed. So... I don't know, girl...'

From beyond the swing doors, Miranda bawls out, 'Angela! Get out there, will you. I'm not paying you two to counsel each other.'

Tiffany bites her lip through her smile, as though thinking the better of saying something. She stands for a moment with a pregnant look on her face before the penny drops for Angela.

'It's a bloke!'

Tiffany almost drops her tray. 'No! Well, yes. No, look, Angela—I *will* tell you...' She squeezes Angela's arm as she walks past her into the dining room.

Quandry

Tiffany leans out through the open window of her daughter's bedroom and breathes in the cool, damp air. The moonlight glimmers on the corrugated roof of Ian's shed and the soft contours of the rambling passionfruit vine cast weird shadows onto the shed wall.

She is not afraid of Ian's eager commitment to the chair project; she knows that she herself is quite incidental to the technological challenge that it represents to him. And yet—he is a man, and she knows it would be unfair of her to stir something in him that he couldn't control.

She draws the curtains and pauses for a while with her hands on the sill. Jane's soft breathing is the only sound to be heard. Tiffany bends and gently repositions her daughter's exposed leg. A trace of the rosy perfume that Sonya wears still lingers. She turns towards the bedside table and spies the book that she must have been reading to Jane before she tucked her in for the night.

Very occasionally, Tiffany would be asked to work

in the evening, and Sonya had made it perfectly clear that she would mind Jane when she came home from school and then take her over to the house when it was time for bed. Jane loved Sonya; the two of them would bake cakes and biscuits, and Sonya was teaching Jane how to knit.

Tiffany bestows a soft kiss on her daughter's cheek then pads to the door. On the bench in the kitchen, on a tray, upon a paper doily with child-sized designs cut into it, sits a teacup with a new teabag on the saucer. Next to it is a small plate with two biscuits covered in plastic wrap.

Sonya had chuckled with delight when she described to Tiffany just how much care and attention Jane put into the presentation of her mother's supper. They had bidden each other good night almost as soon as Tiffany stepped into the hallway, because it was nearly one o'clock.

It had been on the tip of Tiffany's tongue to mention her involvement in the project in the shed—Ian's shed—*your husband's shed!* But, she was tired and felt incapable of shaping a constructive dialogue, so she just squeezed Sonya's hand and looked solemnly into her eyes for a fraction too long.

Balancing her tea, Tiffany lowers herself into the big armchair. She nibbles at the rim of a biscuit and thinks about what she is going to do the next day.

She can't do this without Ian; the two of them are in this together. It's bizarre; it's definitely unconventional, from whatever perspective she looks at it. And it's dangerous. She could lose a lot if things didn't go well.

She sips at her tea.

Is she being selfish? What was that hallucination she had on the veranda a few weeks ago? —as though she was able to peek at some favoured instant in the future. She would be discreet—very discreet, but generous. Not protective and mean—ready and cooperative. She would underplay any embarrassment as mere silliness and immaturity and she would contribute as part of a team—a couple. *Oh, boy... this could get complicated.*

Tiffany imagines herself standing astride the chair.

She will have to give herself a little trim. She gets up and goes to the bathroom.

Technological Frontier

Tiffany shades her eyes against the morning sun as she walks casually back from the street kerb onto the lawn. She casts a last look at the school bus turning the corner, then bends to lavish some unfamiliar attention on a hardy shrub. This is always a quiet time in the street—when children have been whisked away and women are in the kitchen putting on the kettle. She looks up from the brittle banksia and spies the roller door half open. Her mouth is dry and her knees are numb. Tiffany straightens and breaths deeply. It takes just a few seconds for her to glide to the shed and disappear under the roller door.

Ian is enthusiastic. 'The amplitude diodes,' he begins with perfunctory confidence, 'are now in series with the wave generator, so this should allow for a modified sine wave curve, which...' he looks about uncertainly, 'should be a lot more satisfactory.'

'Is Sonya still asleep?'

'Um, yes. How did you know?'

'I didn't see her in the garden this morning. And her bike is under the house.'

Ian drops to his knees and, with his chin resting on

the concrete, looks under the chair. 'Oh, yes,' he grunts, 'she's just having a sleep in.' He toys with something in the confined space. 'Needs a bit of tidying up. The circuit board is a bit exposed.' Ian stands and stretches, his face flushed and a little swollen. 'Oh, don't worry, she never comes here. Seems to think that I need a space to myself—which gives her time to *herself*.' He grins and looks at his hands, wipes them on the front of his shirt, then reaches behind him and searches until his fingers locate the controller on the bench. 'I modified this. So, it's remote now. No lead. You can adjust for a broad or narrow field.' He tenders the controller in an open hand for Tiffany to see.

She skips to Ian's side and searches his face. 'I hope it's not complicated. I can't promise you that I'll be in a receptive mind for complications.'

Ian laughs too boldly. 'No! No... not too...' He scratches his head.

'So,' Tiffany drawls, 'what do I have to twist to take me to the stars and back?'

'Ah,' Ian rubs his nose, 'tracking is with dial... forwards... backwards...' They both peer down into the slot of the chair as something hums and moves in the shadows. 'And this dial is intensity—from mild, through to ah... well, intense.'

Tiffany glimpses in Ian's look the soulful genius of man; the inspiration of the fleeting mind. 'I call it the Thrummer, Ian. Because that's what it sort of feels like... it thrums. Do you think that's an onomatopoeic metaphor? Thrum?'

41

Ian's senses spin. *Wouldn't it be nice to say 'thrum' against her lips.* He sways.

Tiffany puts her hand on his chest and her mouth to his ear. 'We are facing a frontier. We have to be courageous—and sexually impartial. You know what I'm saying?'

Ian nods. He offers Tiffany the controller.

She grasps it lightly. 'Thank you,' she whispers. 'Are you going to close the roller door?'

Ian turns, unfocused, towards the pool of harsh sunlight under the door. As he leans down on the roller door, he hardly hears its squealing, his head is so full. When he turns, Tiffany is stuffing her underwear into the pocket of her skirt.

She bites at her lip, then gives an encouraging smile.

Ian grins back. This is an invasion of his domain that, whilst perhaps imagined once or twice in a moment of fantasy, has rendered him weak and disoriented. Conscious of needing to maintain some sort of momentum, he walks to the bench. He can't allow the moment to collapse—not with Tiffany expecting him to be in charge. He searches the bench for the control unit but can't see it anywhere. Panic surges through him. Then he hears Tiffany's soft voice.

'Looking for this?' She holds out the controller in her hand.

Ian snorts and touches his forehead, 'It's in good hands, I see.' He stands beside her and searches his mind for a suitable cue. 'Well, you'll work it out.'

'We'll work it out, Ian.'

Tiffany looks down and, with a delicate step, straddles the seat, throwing an arm to Ian for balance. She gathers her skirt with one hand and lowers herself to the cool leather. Easing herself into the comfortable contours, she lowers the armrests and places the controller in the newly constructed armrest holder. Her hand hovers over the dial. Then, she turns it resolutely half way around. She surveys the dim interior of the shed with a tilted chin and faraway eyes. The chair is supportive, and the neck rest is far enough back for her head to arch—as though to separate her mind from her body—the experience from existence. A clamorous sexuality enthrals Tiffany's thoughts, and she wriggles into a better position. There's a selfish dimension to this experience that frees her from any physical limitations and any sense of obligation to another. She feels as though her body has a magnificent inertia—an eroticism so gravitational that her surroundings become immutable desires that fall shamelessly to her mind, conferring on her, from a carnal realm, the blessing of a euphoric and physical love...

So, it comes as a bit of a shock, when she re-enters the world, to find that Ian has his face buried between her thighs and that there appears to be smoke coming out of his ears.

At first, she can't speak—her jaw seems to be locked tight.

Ian coughs.

She reaches down and taps him on the back of

his head. 'Ian… Ian… something's wrong… I can smell smoke.'

Ian lifts his head. Wisps of smoke follow him up and curl out from between Tiffany's thighs. Tears and drool drip from his chin onto her skirt.

'Ian—do something! It's electrical. I can smell it.'

He arches back and collapses onto his back with his legs bent behind him. He wipes his face with his sleeve.

Tiffany looks down between her legs at the haze of smoke wafting out of the slot. 'Ian,' she keens, 'what's happening?'

'It's okay… it's okay,' Ian's voice is rough and choked. 'It's just the circuit board. I seem to have dribbled on it.'

Tiffany looks across at her neighbour with a mixture of disgust and alarm. 'It's not going to explode, is it?'

Ian rolls to his side and coughs. 'No. No, it won't explode.' He reaches for the extension lead and whips out the plug. Obliquely, he looks towards the chair. 'Tiff—I'm really sorry. I'm really sorry…' Gathering his knee under his chin, he stares at the floor.

Tiffany eases herself against the backrest and massages her jaw. 'Were you crying?'

He gives a tiny gesture of helplessness.

Tiffany slumps and stares up into the trusses while she recovers her breath. 'Did your tears short-circuit the board?'

Ian is bereft. His hands attempt to convey something before his voice comes through. 'Tiffany—you're beautiful. Not just you—all of you. I mean women—

and no one has ever come into my shed before. I can't explain. I was overcome...'

With a little laugh, Tiffany lurches forward and blows smoke away from her groin. 'It's okay. It's okay.'

Just the occasional creak from the chair intrudes into the silence.

'Oh, Ian. Look at us,' she holds out her hand for a lift. 'Come and help me out of here.'

Groaning with both effort and shame, Ian gets to his feet and takes hold of her hand.

Tiffany heaves out of the chair, shakes loose her skirt and stands against her neighbour. She puts her arms around him and rests her head on his shoulder.

Ian rests his head against Tiffany's but keeps his hands by his side. 'Did it work?'

She nods in his shoulder. 'Uh huh.'

Ian brings up his arms to enfold her. His hands brush over her bare bottom, where the back of her skirt has creased and remained scrunched up. He delicately unfolds the material and lets it fall.

Up at the little window, Sonya's impassive face is visible for a moment before she lets the passionfruit vine drape back against the pane.

Minding Another's Business

Across the street from Ian and Sonya's place, in a ground level, weatherboard house with an uncut lawn, lives Max. In his late twenties, he has pulled a lounge chair up to the window and, with his finger inserted in the blind, is peering through the gap at Ian's shed. Max's back is tattooed with Celtic swirls and knots that run over his shoulder and along his wiry arms all the way to the gleaming Celtic knot ring on his finger. Beyond the ring, beyond the neglected grass, across the road, in dappled sunlight, Sonya makes her way from the shed, behind the passionfruit vine, to the house.

'That bastard,' murmurs Max, 'that miserable, fuckin' bastard.' He settles back in his chair, looking dark.

Bored with the spare time that he has from his ill-fated tattoo parlour, he has taken to idling on the couch and fuming at life. Tiffany's excursions to the shed have come to his attention, and now he has settled in for some serious snooping.

He gropes for the can of beer at his feet.

Tiffany's presence inside the shed for the best part of an hour defies explanation. And Sonya's presence, for an equal time at the little window underneath the rampant passionfruit vine, is too thrilling for words. It leaves him with a meagre handful of expletives with which to articulate his rage.

'That miserable... miserable, fuckin' bastard.'

A thin squealing from outside causes him to lunge forward and pull a gap in the blind. Max squints. Across the street, Tiffany is scuttling under the roller door, and Ian's legs are the last thing to be seen before it squeals closed again.

'Fuckin' bastard,' Max breathes.

Small Town

At the hardware store in town, it's business as usual, and for Ellen, that means that there's too much time spent at the counter looking out at the main street.

Nothing much has changed since she and Ron took over the family business thirty-five years ago. Their marriage, soon after leaving school, and the offer to manage the shop, was considered by the community to have been the best possible outcome when considering the unfortunate prior circumstances. Then, hinted hopes and compounding obligations, the flight of dreams and the impossibility of leaving, left Ellen bound to her place at the counter, and whilst she was justifiably very proud of what she and Ron had achieved with their three sons, she was becoming increasingly unsettled by the way in which circumstance had dictated her life. She wasn't unhappy—but she didn't feel endowed; something had been taken from her, and it wouldn't have mattered where she roamed, she knew intuitively that the best chance she had of finding what she had lost was to remain where she was. Yet, the wait was beginning to feel intolerably long.

A young woman on a bicycle veers across the street and bounces over the kerb onto the footpath just in front of the hardware display window. She pushes down the stand and, from a basket on the handlebars, lifts a small pile of magazines.

A bell tinkles as the front door opens. Sally walks through the aisle up to the counter.

Ron follows behind, wiping his hands on his apron. 'Hello! It's the Pony Express.'

Sally neighs heartily.

Ellen turns, smiles and affects a taken aback frown. 'Is that all?'

Sally peels one thin T.V. guide off the pile and holds it out like a dead fish. 'Not much to it, is there. It'll all fit onto a single sheet soon, if we don't get more business.'

Ellen looks out onto the streetscape. 'Not much to advertise anymore.'

Sally slaps the guides onto the counter. 'Well, you're right about that,' she plucks one from the top and passes it back to Ron, 'I've been told,' and she inclines her head in the direction of the bank building across the street, 'that now is not a good time to start the saddlery. So,' she compresses her lips into a thin white line, 'I'll have to put my plans on hold.'

Ron puts the magazine on the counter and gives Sally a little hug. 'That's too bad, Sal. The time will come—the time will come.'

Sally brightens. 'Not to worry!' She gives a little wave and trots back to the door.

Through the window, Ellen watches her collect her bike and wheel off. On the other side of the street, on the footpath in front of the bakery, Iris is bending over a pavement blackboard, vigorously rubbing out a scrawled 'PASTIES', leaving only 'PIES' and 'SAUSAGE ROLLS'. Her breasts ripple with the movement.

Ellen knows that it is her anger that makes her do this so vehemently. She has witnessed this daily ritual of martyrdom for years—Iris rubbing out the items that have sold out and that she had never wanted to bake in the first place.

With a greying strand of hair fallen across her face, Iris places her hands on her hips and views the street.

Ellen runs her eye over the border of the display window; it's like a screen onto which are played the petty dramas of everyday life in the town. She cants her head to refresh her image and harks back to another time. *I was an artist, once.*

A yellow Triumph Stag coupe pulls up at the footpath. Ellen watches idly as Ian lets himself out and makes his way to the hardware entrance. Her gaze drifts into the distance.

Next to the bakery stands the Empire Fashion House, a fine old Federation edifice built by the Gatton dynasty, the district's earliest settlers. It is the most remarkable feature in a town that has languished for too long. In the arched display windows are exquisite mannequins superbly dressed in Edwardian era fashions, replete with cigarette holders, canes, fans, feather boas and monocles. Lovely examples of Art

Nouveau and Art Deco lamps and other furnishings complement the presentation along with a lush display of drapes and tapestries.

Parked in front of the fashion house, with one wheel mounted on the pavement, is a vintage Rolls-Royce, and placing an envelope behind the windscreen wipers is the long-suffering parking officer. He turns to look at the stone portal that is the entrance to the shop, looks at a nearby signpost, shrugs his shoulders and walks away shaking his head.

A door opens within the portal and a tall, gaunt woman, old and impeccably attired in black, ventures to the edge of the step. She leans forward with an imperious gaze at the departing parking officer. Lifting her hand to her mouth, she attempts, with some difficulty, to insert a slender cigarette holder. She drags deeply and surveys the street. Her ragged make-up is the only outward sign, at least to the townsfolk who have always known her, that her mind is at last relinquishing its iron hold on her body. Her trembling hand again probes about her mouth. She takes another drag before turning to go back inside.

Ellen gives a wan smile. In all the time that Moira Gatton has run the fashion house—at least for as long as anyone can remember—it has rarely made a sale. Whereas Iris despises having to sell to anyone her pies, Moira rejects everyone as being unworthy of owning one of her objets d'art, and the interior has remained a shrine from the time of empires.

Ellen recalls when she was a young high school

student, watching Moira's immaculately made face behind the wheel of the dusty Rolls-Royce as it crunched slowly along the driveway to the teacher's carpark. Moira was the French teacher. She lived alone in a sprawling Edwardian manor house just out of town.

At the back of the Empire Fashion House is a parlour where Moira has occasional guests for afternoon tea. The opulence is mind-boggling. Most of the shop-owners and landed aristocracy have been invited—usually just once. Ellen and Ron sipped from the finest Chelsea china. The atmosphere had been impossibly strained and awkward, and the tea was like tanner's solution.

Ian moves into Ellen's line of sight. 'Good morning, Ellen. Are you lost—in thought.'

'It's the afternoon, Ian'

'Is it already?' He deposits a jumble of hardware onto the counter and spreads it out.

The hardware shop is a place where Ian feels pleasantly comfortable, and it's not just because of the proliferation of building components on the shelves. He is thrilled, ever so little, just to see Ellen. Having known her from childhood, they were good friends during high school.

Being a person of ideas, Ian's mind resides in the future and he rarely makes contact in the here and now. It is Sonya who clothes him in the present, but it was Ellen who undressed him in the past.

He would model for her and she would bully him

into posing stark naked on the picnic table at the lookout on the escarpment above the town. She would study her palette and exclaim that there wasn't enough crimson to do his face. And, the whole time, she would laugh and chatter, while Ian tried to tune in to the subsonic sounds of an approaching car.

Her laughter. He remembers so well.

Ellen waits patiently for Ian to gather his thoughts then decides to provoke him. 'And what are we inventing today?'

Ian has to think about this one, because the thought of the Thrum chair is prominent on his mind, and he has to be careful not to reveal anything—especially to women, who always seem to know what he's thinking. A poised answer...

'Ian?'

'Oh, nothing... much... at all...'

Ellen arches a brow and lowers her eyes. She tallies the cost of the purchases in the account book.

Ian looks at Ellen's still brown hair and lingers on her lovely profile—the side that always catches the light from the window. Everything had changed so suddenly for her, and for years and years Ian would long to be able to make Ellen laugh again. Now, he finds himself perusing the aisles of the hardware store regularly, and Sonya jokes that his passion for inventing is simply a way for him to reacquaint with Ellen. Sonya is very intuitive—and practical—and probably right. Without her presence, Ian's gifts would never have matured. He remembers an industry awards night where he very self-consciously walked back from the podium with a framed certificate in his hands, searching anxiously for his seat next to Sonya—Sonya, who was always happy to discuss hydraulics and bearings with him whenever he was engaged in a project... and a sonic holographic vibrator... built into the seat of a...

The thought of the easychair prompts a change in Ian's perspective, and he lowers his eyes to Ellen's milky cleavage.

She looks up too soon. 'Anything more then, Ian?'

'Ah, no thanks. I was just...'

'Lost in a little fantasy for a moment, were you?' Ellen says, beyond patronising.

There is a brief frisson of eye contact as she hands him his bag.

'See you later, Ellen.' He gives a little wave.

Through the display window, she follows his progress along the footpath and watches him climb into his coupe. *It could have been him— it wouldn't have mattered.*

Reminiscences

At the roadhouse, Ian leans against his beloved roadster and fills it from the bowser. His mouth makes little movements as he recalls his words with Ellen. He snorts softly and chuckles, 'Ellen's tits,' he whispers and shakes his head, 'What's happening to me. After all this time.'

The petrol gurgles noisily. He used to be able to fill up his old Wolseley for less than five bucks. He would leave the college grounds as early as possible and drive to Sonya's house which was in the salubrious part of Brisbane. He would slowly cruise down the little laneway and stop at the kerb just outside her bedroom window. Sonya often chose to climb out of the window just to generate a thrill; her parents were very liberal and open-minded.

One morning, as she slid over the windowsill, her dress caught in the latch and she became stuck halfway down. Ian had come to her rescue and had stood for the longest moment with his arms about her knees and with his face pressed against her underwear before he could lower her to the ground.

He'd been embarrassed for her, but Sonya thought it was hilarious and wouldn't stop laughing about it.

Eventually, after much cooing and cajoling, she got him to smile. But, what lingered in Ian's mind was the softness of her bottom. He never forgot it, and it displaced the longings he had developed for Ellen.

Ian's daydream is broken by Tiffany, standing in front of him in her waitress uniform, supporting her bike and looking at him with a tilted head.

'Oh... hi, Tiffany!' Some fuel spills and he jumps back and holds on to the dripping nozzle with both hands. The shame he feels about his behaviour with Tiffany the day before has not yet been tested, and seeing her standing there, squinting against the mid-day haze, makes him conscious of the awful breach of trust that he has committed. He searches her face. 'Tiffany...'

Tiffany pushes the bike forward so that the front wheel lodges between his trouser legs. She leans forward with a grin. 'Ian, I'm in on this too. You don't have to apologise—unless you were about to tell me that you don't want to go ahead with... with the chair.' Tiffany's face crumples a little with the thought.

'Oh, no! No, no,' Ian turns on the spot and replaces the nozzle. He pulls a length of tissue paper from the dispenser. 'I want to go ahead... I mean, to make a... I fixed it,' he wipes his hands with the tissue, 'I fixed it already. I can help you take it in to your house when... whenever.'

Tiffany beams. She withdraws the bike and looks over at the restaurant. 'I've got to get to work. I'll see you tomorrow.'

Oops

The Triumph turns faster than usual around the leafy street corner, and Ian guns the motor just for fun as he rolls up the driveway into the garage under the house. Full of elation and relief, he hoists himself above the seat and vaults to the ground, not bothering with the car door. Grabbing his bag of hardware, he trots up the front stairs onto the veranda.

Entering the street from the other end is a Harley-Davidson. It idles slowly with an irregular burble towards Ian's house. Nearing the house, the rider steers across the road and parks at the low house with the uncut lawn.

Max unzips his leather vest, lifts off his helmet and takes a long hard look as the screen door closes hesitantly behind Ian.

Ian strides along the hallway to the kitchen. He calls to Sonya with his habitual tweak of dependency, the familiar creases of a smile half-ready. He looks around. With a puzzled frown he opens the back door and stands on the landing, studying the back yard and the clothes line. He treads down the steps, swinging the little bag of hardware. With a bent head, he walks alongside the passionfruit vine, then stops and stares. He runs the last few metres and shoves open the back door of the shed. The light doesn't penetrate far into the disordered gloom, but he can see that the lamp is on. Ian crashes his way forward. He stops. The bag drops from his grip. Draped over the workbench is a rumpled dress. Beside the bench, Sonya, completely naked, is lying in the easychair with her head arched back and her eyes wide. Her hands are trembling and twitching—searching—for the Thrum controller that has fallen out of her reach.

It was not Sonya's intention that Ian should find her like this—naked and speechless in the chair. But, how would he ever live with his indiscretion if she didn't set about sorting things out? She needed to know the facts, and Ian would have been mortified if she had asked him straight out for a turn on it.

Now she has lost control of the thing and she can't tell shame from sensation, erotic from chaotic, and the dark vault of unconsciousness that she can feel pending is both welcome and a nuisance.

Ian's stricken face comes into view. Sonya tries to say something. She can feel him cradling her head. His body jerks. The relentless pulsing that has taken over her body stops. Ian has pulled out the power cord. Sonya can feel his face pressing against her, but she can't articulate her apology. She faints.

Unbelievable

Max walks into the lounge and pops open a beer. He takes a swig and puts it next to the chair pulled up to the window. He settles back and lights a cigarette, draws heavily on it, then sits forward and pulls down a gap in the blind.

It's not as though Max has always had it in for Ian. Ian's a bloke who keeps pretty much to himself, but that, if the truth be told, is part of what aggravates Max—the fact that Ian is perfectly happy with himself.

Now, with a cigarette on his lip and a finger in the blind, he is awaiting the outcome of the confrontation that he feels certain is going on between Ian and Sonya inside the shed. He'd seen Sonya striding towards the shed earlier on, when Ian's Triumph had barely left the street. She was in there for so long that he'd run out of cigarettes and he had nipped down to the shop to buy another packet.

He peers out, looks left and right, then reaches down for his beer. He takes a long pull then sets about unzipping his boots.

Whilst it is obvious that Max is born to ride, he has the unmistakable aura of one destined to lose, but it is not for a lack of talent. On the walls around the room are many brilliant art works, all of them elegantly signed—Max.

He places his boots neatly by the wall, sits forward again and opens a slit. He is about to take another swig, when he abruptly thrusts forward. His other hand comes up to widen the gap in the blinds.

Beyond the blue of the tattoos on Max's arm, and across the expanse of afternoon sunlight, Ian is walking behind the trellised passionfruit. Over his shoulder is an enormous bundle covered in brown canvas. Even behind the rampant vine, Max can quite clearly distinguish the dangling arms and legs of a body.

He issues another paroxysm of swearing. 'Fuckin' hell. Oh, fuckin' hell! What's he done?' He viciously runs his hand down the blind and bolts upright. 'What's he done?' he keens. He turns away from the window and bites at his knuckles. Overwrought with horror, he mutters and cries and kicks at the furniture. 'Jesus! Oh, Jesus—what now? What the fuck now?' He flails his arms about, grabbing at nothing and kicking savagely.

Max is strangling the air, when he hears a noise. He cocks his head towards the window and rushes over. He reefs down a gap in the blinds and pushes his face against it.

Out on the lawn, Phoebe slams the door of her car and strides to the porch.

Max lets his hand slide from the blinds. With uncertain steps, he moves towards the front door and stands there hugging himself, quivering, his face streaked with tears.

Phoebe lets herself in. She recoils in alarm when she sees Max right near the door. 'Max! What are you doing?'

He tries to speak, but all he can manage is some squeaks and sobs.

Phoebe edges up to him, then looks behind her at the lounge chair—the cigarette lying smoking on the floor—the beer spilled on the carpet. 'Max... what have you been doing?' She walks around and picks up the cigarette. She eyes him as she sniffs it.

Max's voice is barely audible, 'Phoebe... he's killed her.'

Phoebe's tired face sinks. She exhales a contemptuous sigh. 'What?'

'That fucking, miserable bastard has killed her, Phoebes,' Max makes an emphatic nod in the direction of the street.

Phoebe stares at her tattooed boyfriend. Her arms go limp and her hands fall open. Her handbag thuds on the carpet. She drops her head and starts to sob. 'Oh, Max...'

Resolute

The Zodiac has not dealt favourably with Phoebe in the last few years. Her return to the town with an art student boyfriend, and the opening of the Glamorama, her hair salon, at first caused great excitement. She trumpeted her arrival with glossy flyers for the new business, housed in the rambling old emporium in the main street of town.

Sadly, the intervening years between her leaving for the Big Smoke, and her return with a head full of ideas, coincided with a collapse in rural vitality. The Glamorama's young clientele began to depart town to find work elsewhere. Phoebe's brand of chic didn't appeal to older, rural women, and gradually the dream became a monotonous reality.

And now Max is raving about murder.

Phoebe knocks softly on the leadlight of Ian and Sonya's front door and lets the screen door squeal shut. From the high veranda, she looks over at her house and imagines Max hunkered against the loungeroom wall with his face in his hands. He'd told her everything he'd seen and had slid down against the wall looking inconsolable.

Phoebe found herself sitting in the lounge chair staring at the blinds, thinking about Max—not Ian—not Sonya. She and Max had been so much in love; improbably, they had found each other through the swirling cosmos.

The door opens inwards and Ian walks out onto the threshold, pushing open the screen door.

'Hello, Phoebe,' he says with surprise and warmth.

Phoebe searches Ian's open face. 'Hello, Ian,' she replies tonelessly. She spends every day, secretly, and with the aid of mirrors, studying people's faces from all angles and distances. She can tell that Ian is no more capable of murder than Max is. There is nothing sinister here. But, she owes it to Max—and Sonya, who has always treated her with such kindness. 'Could I speak to Sonya, please? I was just wondering if she was thinking about getting her hair done... soon... at all...'

Ian nods agreeably as he holds on to the flyscreen door. 'Ah, yes. Her hair. Um...' he steps back through the doorway and turns to look inside. 'She's... I don't know... not feeling, ah, that well... just at the moment.'

'Oh.' Phoebe takes a quick look behind her at her house.

They stand briefly in a silent impasse.

'I'd really like to see her... *have* to see her—if that's okay?'

'Of course, Phoebe—come through.'

She pulls the flyscreen door wide and brushes close by Ian. She can smell the heat and perspiration on his body.

'She's asleep.' He indicates the bedroom door and stands aside to let Phoebe in.

Phoebe stands by the bed. Sonya looks so serene, with a sheet to her chin and her arms, uncovered, by her side. Her cheeks are quite flushed and rosy, and there is the tiniest hint of a smile on her mouth. Phoebe reaches for Sonya's hand and holds it delicately at the wrist. The pulse is strong and slow. As she allows her neighbour's hand to slide to the bed, Sonya gives Phoebe's hand a light squeeze, and the smile broadens ever so slightly. The tears begin to well in Phoebe's eyes. She looks down at the older woman and wonders how it is that one soul can do so much good. Closing her eyes, she squeezes a teardrop onto the sheet in a silent supplication for help.

Ian backs softly out of the room, but Phoebe is turning around already and gives him an anguished smile.

'Thank you, Ian,' she whispers.

He nods uncertainly.

Phoebe brushes by him. 'I hope she feels better soon.'

'Oh, I'm sure she will, Phoebe. She just overdid it a bit today—she'll be fine.'

From the veranda rail, Ian follows Phoebe's return to her house and wonders about the unearthly powers of communication that women seem to possess.

Termination

Phoebe storms through the open front door and goes straight to the kitchen.

Max trails behind her and watches her yank open the fridge door. Sensing that the landscape has somehow altered, he slides his hands into his back pockets and leans against the door jamb, hoping to diffuse anything awkward. 'What did you find out?'

Crossing the road was all the time needed for Phoebe to realise that it is over with Max, and that there is no easy way to do this but to grab a beer out of the fridge and sit down and begin the ending. Except that she can't believe how foolish Max has been and just how much his life has degenerated. So, instead of a calmly delivered ultimatum, she explodes in fury.

Phoebe wrings the cap off her beer and hurls it at Max. 'I've found out, Max, that you're a fucking idiot! There's nothing wrong with her—she's perfect!' She looks around for a chair, plonks herself down and takes a long swig. 'She's just a little tired, Max. She's resting in bed.' She has another pull and looks at her soon-to-be ex staring vacantly at the wall. 'Too much time, Max. Too much time and not enough to do...'

She is going somewhere with this but decides to have another mouthful.

Max fidgets and tries to compose himself. 'Did you see any bruises?'

Phoebe nearly chokes on her beer. 'Fucking hell, Max! I told you—she's perfect—there's nothing wrong with her. What were you expecting? They're our neighbours—older, happily married, boring, helpful. Why in God's name would he want to kill her? What on earth have you seen that would lead you to that conclusion?'

Max is a little frightened of Phoebe's vehemence. 'It's just... I've seen things, Phoebes... and the chick across the road...'

'*The chick across!* Right, that's it!' Phoebe propels herself off the chair and strides past Max to the bedroom. She slams the door.

Max straightens and walks into the lounge. It's late afternoon and the room has become dark. Max goes to the lounge chair in front of the window and sinks into it. On an impulse, he reaches out and pulls a gap in the blinds. His arm seems black with tattoos and the silver knot gleams dully on his finger.

Out on the lawn, the chrome on his Harley-Davidson is reflecting the last of the golden light. Beyond the bike, on the other side of the street, the shed seems bland and innocuous.

Max nods his head ever so slightly.

66

Out With a Whimper

The morning's shadows are retreating from the roadway towards the veranda posts outside the Glamorama. Phoebe's salon now takes up just a corner inside the huge, old emporium. The echo inside is eerie. Her clients speak in hushed tones, because a laugh or a strident word will ring for long enough to be embarrassing. When the business was going well, the space seemed to absorb music and noise, and customers naturally lost their inhibitions. Now, every sound taunts Phoebe. Even the clicking of scissors sounds like the seconds of eternity.

Phoebe puts down the comb and cups Hannah's mauve curls with her hands. She darts a glance to the mirror and catches her client passively toying with her wedding ring, turning it over and over. 'How's that, Hannah?'

'Hmm? Oh, that's lovely, Phoebe.'

Phoebe whisks at Hannah's shoulders with a brush as they regard each other in the mirror. 'Don't forget to put the ring back on your finger.'

A sound from the footpath distracts them.

Ian pops his head in the doorway. 'Hi, Phoebe,'

he says with a cheery wave, 'Sonya said to make it for tomorrow. And, she wants the works—whatever that may be.'

'She's feeling better, then?' Phoebe replies with a wistful smile.

'Much better... yep...' Ian lingers and fidgets, then waves goodbye.

Phoebe goes to the counter where Hannah is opening her purse. They smile tightly at each other and exchange a few constrained pleasantries.

When the sound of Hannah's footsteps has receded from the doorway, Phoebe scans the room as though for one last time. On the walls of the salon are faded and curling posters of young models with outrageous hairstyles and extreme make-up. To one side, cluttering a bench and partly obscuring a wall mirror, is a pile of beauty paraphernalia obviously not in current use. Phoebe takes one of the boxes in her hands and looks at herself in the clear segment of the mirror. She is crying quietly. This is not how she imagined her life would be when she came back to the town.

Reflected in the mirror is the Glamorama's display window, and through to the other side of the street, tucked away between a shop for lease and the veterinarian's practice, is a recessed entrance with a steel door. Painted on the door is a sword-brandishing warrior, and above, is emblazoned in curls and knots, CELTIC BODY ART. Dangling from the slide bolt is a huge padlock. Phoebe has been down the bleak, brick corridor behind the door many times. The dilapidated storeroom that it leads to had been club headquarters for the region's ragtag gang of bikers.

Max's arrival in town had stirred a lot of interest. His ability as an artist and his bona fides in the form of his Harley-Davidson, soon had him admitted into the inner sanctum of a very sincere bunch of farm hands and stockmen whose bodies became Max's canvas, and who happily parted with a lot of money after agonising hours on a table. But, the economic crisis bit deep, and a bikie without a job soon becomes a bikie without a bike. One day, the roaring phalanx left town, leaving Max's Harley alone to rumble through the streets.

Phoebe realises that there'll be no more trips with Max. Her eyes refocus on her image in the mirror.

Slueth

Max is dressed to make his exit. But, there remains one thing to do before he rides out of town. In full leathers, he is prowling about in the gloom of Ian's shed, scanning the bench tops, being careful not to upset anything. His gloved hands linger on machine tools and strange constructions. He is searching for something— some *thing,* to explain what he has witnessed over the last few weeks.

What he sees seems innocent enough—the product of years of tinkering to find engineering solutions. Max knows it's neither fair nor reasonable to single out Ian to vent his frustrations.

The sudden realisation of what he has been reduced to doing hits him and he steadies himself against the bench. The darkness is too close a metaphor for his life at this moment and he scrabbles to find the switch for the table lamp. The lamp is aimed down, and the light floods the floor. Leaning with his knuckles on the bench, Max breathes deeply and lowers his chin to his chest, allowing his eyes to stare dully towards the glow coming from the bright yellow leather chair.

The sunny reflection restores interest in Max's eyes

and, with a bemused furrow on his brow, he kneels for a closer look. His hand meets something soft lying on the floor against the bench. He delicately holds it out. It's a pair of women's underpants—sensible ones.

Still squatting, he leans back against the bench and ponders the object in his grip. Unconsciously, he rubs the material between his fingers. His eyes stray to the chair, unusual in its configuration and with a strange slot in the seat. Max jerks forward and peers into the space at the mechanisms just visible in the shadows. He runs his fingers along the neatly sewn edge as he looks about. His eyes follow the electrical lead that runs away from the chair to a power-board. Next to the board is a small remote-control unit, and as Max reaches over to grasp it, he sees that he still has the underwear in his hand. His attention alternates between the material and the strange panel on the remote.

Max pales. He drops the garment. Slowly he rises. A gradual realisation works on his face, and when the connections are finally made, he is appalled. Transfixed with horror, his gaze fixes on the slot in the chair.

He is in the lair of a pervert.

Max looks behind him. The back door is closed, as he had left it. It's very quiet. He'll hear the Triumph's sporty note a mile off. He rests on the bench edge and hooks his thumbs into the belt loops of his leathers. The remote module is still on the floor, black and sinister— like a rogue cell waiting for its cue to metastasise. Max unzips a boot.

How many other projects are there in the shed

that are weird—suspended in the trusses—up against the walls—lodged behind the door—in shelves and drawers? Why the darkness? Only one tiny window, and that almost completely covered by the passionfruit vine. And no lights, at least none that work, apart from the table lamp. And the roller door that never opens—except lately, to admit his neighbour, Tennille or Crystal or whatever her name is. Did she sit in this chair? Was she told to? Obviously not—she was at liberty to come and go—ducking under the roller door first thing in the morning and departing the same way with a little wave an hour later.

Max's eyes rove about the room—to the work lamp, throwing a yellow sheen onto his riding boots sitting neatly side by side on the workbench—to his leather pants folded next to the boots—to his black briefs and gloves draped over the edge of the bench top.

Max moves and stands astride the chair. Wearing only his leather vest, he zips it right up. His face is expressionless as he lowers himself to meet the seat, his genitals disappearing into the slot. In his hand is the remote control and, with a moment's hesitation, he turns the dial.

Max grins with revelatory triumph. Then his visage flickers. Something is wrong.

He looks at the dial and carefully turns it all the way around. He looks puzzled. He turns the other dial with studious deliberation, all the way around. He shakes the controller and sits there with confusion on his face.

He spies the electrical plug lying next to the power-board. Max smirks. He places the controller on the floor and reaches over and picks up the plug. He pulls the power-board next to the chair, lines up the plug with the socket, and rams the plug home.

It Never Ends

Ian blips the throttle and grins smugly at the garrulous trumpeting of the Triumph's exhaust echoing off the houses. In a bag beside him he has Sonya's favourite liqueur chocolates. As he steers into the driveway, he can already feel the softness of her shoulder. All the explaining has been done; Sonya knew everything anyway, so now is the time for love and relief.

He cuts the engine and sits for a moment. There is something in the firmament that he definitely isn't tapping into; circumstances are always so much more of a surprise for him than anyone else.

He clutches the bag and vaults over the car door. With his head down, he trips up the stairs, thinking about the hour he had sat on the end of the bed listening to Sonya as she half-whispered her story. She had been utterly shocked. To see her husband—her predictably proper husband—with his head buried in another woman's thighs, had almost caused her to swoon with astonishment. And, the memory of him clutching at her hips and emerging, crying and dishevelled, would have never ever reconciled with her if it hadn't been for her own experience in the chair.

Ian sat, palled with ignominy, listening to his beating heart and hoping that he would soon be able to stroke the foot that had conveniently appeared from under the quilt near his hand. It wasn't long before he *was* stroking Sonya's foot—and she asked him whether he did love her more than their pretty neighbour—and he said that, yes, he truly did—which made her feel quite delighted, because, Tiffany, she said, was indeed alluring, and that kind of confirmed the magnitude of their love for each other after all these years—to which Ian replied, that it was exactly because of the years that he loved Sonya so much—which made her rue even more, whilst gently prodding his buttock with her foot, the fact that she had interfered with his project.

This outcome was something that pleasantly surprised Ian and generated an ample magnanimity—whilst completely overlooking the fact that Sonya had once again set things right without even a whiff of censure.

Ian pauses at the top of the stairs and glances over to Phoebe's house. A lump comes to his throat and he feels a welling of emotion that he can't explain. Somehow, it feels as though he is being awakened to a mystery—something that has either eluded him or been kept a secret. He pulls slowly at the squeaking screen door. An image, of soft shadows and arcs of downy skin, dances in his mind; he feels filled with a sensuality that he knows he must never take for granted. He lets the door close.

Sonya is sitting in an armchair with two footstools

in front of her, each some distance apart. She is resting her calves on them with her legs splayed slightly. She looks up from the television as Ian enters.

He bends and kisses her gently and produces the chocolates from behind his back.

Sonya gives a little squeal and reaches up and strokes Ian's neck.

He massages her knee and looks over at the television. The picture is distorted and grainy. 'What's wrong with the telly, love?'

Sonya shakes her head. 'I don't know, Ian. It started doing it about two or three minutes ago. I tried adjusting it with the remote...'

Ian slowly straightens, his face blank. He turns and looks at a point beyond the wall, then heads towards the kitchen. Pushing open the screen door, he trips quickly down the stairs.

The passionfruit tendrils flick at his face as he runs to the shed. He can't believe that the saga of the sonic chair has not yet ended. Humans stray to all manner of convolutions; the vine has a simple agenda—to convert sunlight into food in its deep, green leaves— and to grow little passionfruit.

Ian swings himself bodily into the back door of the shed. He lurches inside as the door crashes against the garden tools stacked in the corner. It is completely dark inside, but Ian knows the layout and scrambles quickly forward. The light from the doorway doesn't reach the floor next to the bench, but that is where Ian stops and stoops. His eyes adjust to the gloom.

Max is stretched out in the chair, his breath coming in short gasps, his hands patting and groping by the side of the chair, searching.

Ian reaches across Max's twitching body and reefs the electrical plug out of the socket.

Max groans loudly and slumps to one side.

The table lamp is lying smashed beside the bench and there is glass on the floor.

Ian half rises. He needs some light. He steps over Max and bends down to the roller door. He jerks it open in stages to about hip height. A movement outside draws his attention. In the sunlight, he spies Tiffany's dress and her tanned legs. He calls out to her in a harsh whisper. 'Tiffany! Give us a hand here, will you.'

Tiffany comes closer to the door and bends to look underneath. Her hands are to her mouth, her brow creased with dread.

Ian beckons with a wave of his hand. 'C'mon. Help me get him up. Watch out for the glass.'

Tiffany hesitates then looks behind her, up and down the street. She scampers under the roller door, but can't bring herself to come any closer when she sees Max, clothed in only his leather vest, huffing and puffing strenuously, with spittle all over his chin.

'Oh, God,' her voice is a soft squeal. 'Ian, what's happened?'

Ian grabs Max gently around the neck and pulls him upright in the chair. He looks down at Max's nakedness, then at Tiffany's frightened eyes. He starts to say something but changes his mind.

Tiffany spies the controller on the floor and gingerly picks it up. The dials are turned to maximum. She reaches over and gives it to Ian. 'Do you want me to get Sonya?'

Ian's eyes fall away. He nods his head.

Tears

Max is lying on the sofa in the lounge room of his house. A blanket comes right up to his chin and his head is supported by a large, soft pillow. His eyes are closed, and the twilight that manages to get past the blind makes his face look grey.

Phoebe, teary-eyed and looking very isolated, sits at Max's head end in a kitchen chair against the wall. Facing them, in a lounge chair, Tiffany slumps awkwardly, looking up at the ceiling. Next to her, Ian is poised on the edge of his chair, leaning forward with his elbows on his knees, clasping his hands and looking at the floor. Right beside him, on a kitchen chair, is Sonya.

An occasional sniff from Phoebe breaks the silence.

Max has only the tiniest capacity for vitriol—the chair has taken him to the edge. He is utterly dissipated. As though it wasn't bad enough that his life was disintegrating, the spasms in his loins remind him that his circumstances have now become unequivocally humiliating. That he has been exposed to the whole neighbourhood in a most embarrassing and helpless way is all Ian's fault. It makes him feel savage enough to want to kill him. He withdraws his hand from under the blanket and, though his eyes remain closed, he makes a small beckoning gesture in Ian's direction.

Ian rocks forward from the lounge chair and stoops, with his hands on his knees, next to the sofa.

Again, Max beckons him closer.

Ian places a hand on the sofa armrest and lowers his ear towards Max's mouth.

Still with his eyes closed, Max reaches up for the nape of Ian's neck. He draws him downward in an awkward embrace. He raises his mouth to Ian's cheek.

Ian gropes for support, finally crumpling against the sofa as Max's arm hooks around Ian's neck.

Max's eyes flash open. He summons all his strength and snarls in Ian's ear, 'If I can't ride my bike… after this… I'll fuckin' kill you.'

Ian, red in the face from the constriction of Max's grip, stares at the floor.

Ian

I realised that I—actually, all of us—had reached a nadir unique even in our little town. I felt that I had lured innocent people into some sort of sex trap. I was on the way to becoming seriously depressed if it hadn't been for the fact that Sonya and Tiffany continued using the chair behind my back—in the interests of research, apparently.

However, at this moment, Phoebe hated us all—we'd had to tell her everything. She couldn't believe it, but there was no denying the fact that Max was lying there with balls the size of mangoes.

Phoebe started making plans for leaving. Max disappeared—and, I can tell you, that gave me a lot of anxiety. I didn't want to work in the shed—there was nothing to do in the house—there was not enough to do in town. I felt rather vulnerable and ineffectual.

When I did finally see Max, I was on the side of the road, miles out of town, with only Moira Gatton to help me.

But, what is important is that Tiffany had the courage to talk to Phoebe, and that that, and the chair, brought us all together.

Another Lick

It is a Saturday morning and the main street of town is relatively busy. The townsfolk go about their errands in a set and habitual way. Country towns pulse to a slower rhythm, no doubt, but something in the presentation of the shops—the careless displays, worn paint and dark interiors—bespeak a want of vitality.

Moving amongst the turgid throng of pedestrians are Tiffany and Jane, hand in hand, window-shopping in animated conversation. They continue their sunny excursion until they come to the entrance of the Glamorama where Jane suddenly rushes forward and stands spellbound in front of a row of tables set out on the footpath. On them is for sale, very cheaply, all the salon's beauty treatment paraphernalia: make-up kits, waxing treatments, gels, creams, hair-care products, depilatory concoctions—the lot. Jane is fascinated and holds up a make-up kit to her mother.

Tiffany gazes across the tables, through the display window, into the darkness of the old emporium.

Jane tugs at her mother's dress and proffers her treasure.

But, Tiffany is in a world of her own at this moment.

She searches the interior with a dreadful intensity. Mechanically, she takes the make-up kit from Jane's hands.

Jane's eyes widen. She reaches into her mother's handbag and extracts Tiffany's purse.

Tiffany breaks her gaze into the Glamorama and deals with her daughter's demands.

Just as Jane, clutching her kit, is about to rush into the shop with a fist full of money, Phoebe appears in the doorway, her arms tightly folded.

Jane carefully negotiates the few steps leading up to the doorway, squeezes past Phoebe, and disappears inside.

The two women confront each other for an awkward while until Jane reappears at Phoebe's side and holds up her money. Phoebe drags her eyes from Tiffany and looks down at Jane's clutched hand. With reluctance, she brings her hands together.

Jane gleefully drops her bundle into Phoebe's cupped hands, says thank you, and hops down to the pavement.

Tiffany gathers her daughter and looks away. Mother and daughter walk on.

At the bottom end of town there is a park where the monthly car-boot market is in progress. Jane scampers off amongst the tents and stalls while Tiffany walks to a bench seat underneath a huge fig tree. Without focusing, she gathers her things beside her and bites at her lower lip. She knows that in a small town one's past is never far behind, and she would never forgive herself if she didn't try to mend things, even if it meant having to explain an impossibly bizarre situation to a resolutely unforgiving person. She stands and looks about. Spying Jane, she calls to her and beckons her over.

The two of them converse closely. Tiffany extracts some coins from her purse. Then, with a purposeful peck on her mother's cheek, Jane turns away and skips towards the home-made ice-cream stall. Tiffany takes some deep breaths and walks determinedly back up the street.

Inside the Glamorama, Phoebe, with a hairclip in her mouth, concentrates on shaping Janice's hair.

Janice, aged and perceptive, intuitively steers the conversation in the direction of a common enemy. 'Who will I get to do my hair when you go, Phoebe dear?'

Phoebe removes the clip. 'Denise will do it.'

Janice purses her lips ever so slightly. In the mirror, she watches the play of the scissors over her hair. The tension in Phoebe's body is causing a tremor in her hands, and it started when that new young woman walked into the salon and, without so much as a nod, made directly for the settee at the rear of the room. 'Hah! Denise,' Janice scoffs, keeping an eye on the mirror where she can see the newcomer seated on the edge of the cushion with her hands clasped between her knees, 'she makes everybody look like a meringue. I don't know what I'll do without you.'

84

Phoebe has never felt so hurt. For months and months, the town seemed to be conspiring against her. The customers that were always so happy to see her have simply disappeared, and no amount of rational consideration about the rural slump can diminish the feeling that it is somehow her fault. And now, Max has fallen apart—neglecting his tattoo parlour, spending too long at home, neglecting himself—her! And worse, the neighbours she thought she could trust are involved with some sort of sex machine that has completely ridiculed and humiliated both Max and her.

Phoebe flicks the apron away from Janice's shoulders and vigorously brushes her clothing.

Sitting very still, Janice glances at Phoebe's tearing eyes. 'Phoebe, dear... what's the matter?'

Phoebe shakes her head. Then, with a quick dart in the direction of the settee, she sniffs and composes herself. 'Next time, Janice.'

Janice levers herself from the chair. 'Well... I do hope there is a next time.'

The two of them walk to the counter.

As Janice reaches across to pay, she hangs on to the money and says in a low voice, 'Whoever she is, Phoebe, I can see a lot of contrition. Make it work, for both of you—whatever it is.'

Phoebe's gaze stays fixed on the counter top.

Releasing her hold on the money, Janice turns and walks carefully down the steps and out of the salon.

In the dimness of the back reaches of the emporium, Tiffany stands and moves to the counter. Though she is frightened and unsure, her desperate need to make amends pushes her onward.

Phoebe watches her with a lowered head.

Reaching the counter, Tiffany runs her fingers over the edge. 'Phoebe...' she begins, but in Phoebe's face there is so much emotion that Tiffany halts in mid-breath.

Phoebe hisses, 'What could you possibly have to say?'

Tiffany is very aware of just how much she wants to say, but she can't rush. This she must do ever so gently. 'I want you to give me the chance to say something terribly, terribly important, Phoebe. I'm asking you, if you'll hear what I have to tell you.'

The two of them regard each other in the echoing stillness of the emporium.

Outside, Jane has appeared, carefully licking her ice-cream. She cups her hands as best she can and peers through the display window, leaving a round blotch of ice-cream on the glass. Intuitively recognising a tedious situation, she makes her way to the steps and settles on the bottom one. A stray dog lopes from the roadway onto the footpath and pants expectantly near her. She breaks off the soggy bottom of her cone and throws it to the dog.

Inside, the two women separate from their conversation. Tiffany trails her hand across the counter, then goes down the steps to the footpath.

Jane looks up and proffers her now much melted ice-cream for her mother to lick.

Past Caring

Little motes of dust float through the yellow rays of sunlight and, through half closed eyes, tired from worry and now sleepy with resignation, Phoebe lets herself relax in the Thrum chair. Her hand is limp over the controller, and she allows Tiffany's fingers to manipulate hers.

With an arm around Phoebe and with her mouth right by her ear, Tiffany says the things that she hopes will change everything. 'We'll start slowly... very slowly,' she says in a low voice. 'When you're ready, you can rotate the dial, ever so little. It will make you relax... you'll feel lovely... and I'll be here the whole time.'

Phoebe's breathing slows. She thinks about her drive home—only two minutes and not nearly enough time to make up her mind. Tiffany had been so full of remorse, and simultaneously her request had been so outrageous, that Phoebe didn't know what to think. She felt so alone, that she stayed on at the Glamorama, sipping on her cup of tea and staring out onto the quietening street.

When she got home, the house was dismal—full of unrealised dreams. She showered and cried. She towelled herself and looked brave in the mirror. She dressed up, she dressed down. She didn't know what to do, but tempting fate was better than crying at the table, so she slipped on a skirt, marched out of the front door and crossed over to Tiffany's place as she had been asked to.

The sun wasn't far off setting, and her long shadow on the rough lawn gave her the courage to believe that there might be another incarnation for her if she would put aside her anger. Tiffany had left the front door open and Phoebe felt that her leather heels made enough noise as she crossed the veranda for her to go right in without knocking. Tiffany's house, simple and airy inside, sent Phoebe a rush of tiny subliminal messages about the order and nature of things, and the malice in her heart began to evaporate. Tiffany's voice had beckoned her from the sunroom. The sight of the yellow chair almost made her turn back—it looked so eerily innocuous, yet, in the waning sunlight, so incandescently dangerous. But, Tiffany's soothing words had allayed her doubts.

And now, in an emotional capitulation, Phoebe has one hand on the controller and the other clutching her underpants. Each breath is a sigh, and what had at first seemed bizarre, has now become wonderful. The last red rays of the afternoon seem to modulate into a textural energy, brassy and percussive, then strident and dominant, and gradually, a vast plaintive ecstasy enthrals her sensory horizons. Her hand comes off the controller and, with irrepressible exhilaration, she runs her fingers through her hair, arches her neck and rolls her head from side to side.

Tiffany slides her arm off the backrest and hugs Phoebe's shoulders. She reaches down and very slowly rotates the Thrum control to a lower setting. Her head falls against Phoebe's neck. A tear runs down her cheek. She kisses the joyous curl on Phoebe's lips.

*   *   *

Newly Upholestered

Sonya, radiant and smiling, balances a tray with tea for four as she walks past the rambling passionfruit vine towards the shed. Among the lustrous leaves hang many shiny, freckled passionfruit, just becoming purple. The teapot is fat and bountiful, and the cups, upside down on their saucers, look like porcelain eggs about to hatch. With a cautious glance, Sonya negotiates the threshold of the shed door and enters.

Inside it is light, and all the clutter of past projects is gone. The benches are bare, the walls are beige and nothing at all hangs from the roof trusses. There are new lights installed. The concrete floor has a covering of ivory-patterned linoleum, and the old roller door has been replaced with a new one.

Tiffany and Phoebe are seated together on one of the bench tops with Ian seated next to them on another bench.

Sonya places the tea tray next to Ian who rocks off the bench and turns to stand in the middle of the room next to a hairdresser's chair, beautifully upholstered in sun yellow, soft leather.

'Okay,' he begins intrepidly, 'the chair is adjustable

like this...' he tilts the head rest up and down, 'and like that...' he lowers the backrest. 'Just the usual. But this,' he points to a lever by the side of the seat, 'is the adjustment that concerns us... well, you... you know what I mean.'

The three women start laughing and Phoebe calls out, 'More details, Ian—more details.'

'So, what *does* it do?' Tiffany says, hugging herself with anticipation.

It has only taken a few seconds and a handful of words for Ian to realise that this new project is not about engineering, but about people. And in such a milieu, Ian is happy to take a back seat to—well, just about anyone. For him, it is a revelation to see other people interacting so vigorously and sincerely. It is a beauty that has often escaped his attention. To see Sonya and Tiffany and Phoebe so intimately happy fills him with relief.

Ian rivets his eyes to the floor. 'Well, if you girls can restrain yourselves—this lever opens up the slot.' He demonstrates. A neatly closed seam in the chair seat magically opens to reveal the dull sheen on the lens of the Thrum machine. 'See? Open... closed...'

The women ooh and ahh and wriggle forward on the bench.

Ian's poise is restored. 'Now, the sonic pulse device has been improved. It has ah... better penetration properties, a bit like ultra-sound, in a way, but in a much lower frequency, so... the point is, that it is not necessary to be er, naked, to um, fully appreciate the ah, benefits of the chair.'

Phoebe and Tiffany exchange sly grins, Sonya is smiling broadly, and Ian is perspiring freely. He massages the bridge of his nose.

'In addition to the controls with which you are familiar—now located here,' he points to a place at the junction of the seat and backrest, 'there is another feature, operated with this toggle switch just here, that is a sonic tilt adjustment. This is Sonya's idea.'

'Way to go, Sonya!' Tiffany and Phoebe chorus.

Sonya reddens.

Phoebe thrusts up an arm. 'So, who's having first go?'

Amid the laughter and banter, Phoebe is suddenly serious, and a frown pulls at her brow. The others turn to her.

'I don't have many young customers. Most of my clients are older.' She gives an apologetic shrug towards Sonya. 'Too many of my younger clients have left town—so, I don't know how successful it will be. I've gained quite a reputation for my perms.'

Tiffany leans forward to face her neighbour. 'It will work, Phoebe—just in the same way that word got around about your perms, well, the word will get around about the chair.'

Ian's carefully nurtured gravitas falls. 'But, you don't seriously expect people to be chatting about the Thrum chair on every street corner, do you?' He looks about for confirmation.

'Not ordinary people, Ian,' says Sonya patiently,

'women—and you know nothing of women's communication network. And, Phoebe, if you're worried about older people using the chair, it's not really that different from a body massage; older people have got muscles and nerves... and sexual parts—even if they haven't been stimulated in living memory.'

The girls burst out laughing.

Ian reddens.

Sonya lifts her foot up into Ian's crotch from where she is seated on the bench close by him. 'And I'm not talking about us, Ian.'

Tiffany and Phoebe jump down from the bench and confer affectionate hugs on Ian.

Out through the newly cleaned window, a fat ripening passionfruit dangles inertly from its slender stalk, the first wrinkles making it appear like a goddess of ancient times.

Collusion

The old emporium was built in a time when the community felt inspired to create beauty. In times of harshness and austerity for many, the finely worked wrought iron columns gracing the veranda were the reward that one could share in for having toiled so hard. Most buildings, from government offices to hotels and emporiums, decorated with intricate lace panels and delicate frieze brackets, bestowed a thrill of importance upon the visitor, through the grandeur and magnificence of their architecture.

For Phoebe, Tiffany, Sonya and Ian, refurbishing the Glamorama is reacquainting them with a bygone era, letting them feel something of the majesty of lives past. And in each moment of eye contact, there is the frisson of knowing that what they are embarking on would be scandalous in any generation.

Ian is quite aware of the gravity of history—that urge to conform. Of course, all along, people have made spectacular departures from the norm, but he's thinking more of the fundamental morals that underpin society—the innate ethical blueprint. Individuals rarely make radical departures from their sense of humanity, except as an aberration in times of conflict, but Ian is becoming very conscious of the fact that what they are doing might be extremely unethical. He awaits the first encounter with the Thrum chair more with concern than curiosity. How will their collusion be interpreted by future generations? Or Janice's generation, for that matter...

Loquacious

'Hello, Janice, how are you this morning?' Phoebe guides Janice to the gleaming handrail so that she can better ascend the stairs.

'I'm well, dear, thank you,' Janice replies as she surveys the renovated foyer with amazement. 'My goodness—is all this for somebody else, or have you decided to stay?'

Phoebe positions herself beside the old lady. Together they admire the remodelling. 'I've decided to stay.'

'Oh, good for you, dear,' Janice says, throwing a hearty punch at Phoebe's shoulder. 'You're not expecting me to change my habits though, are you?'

Phoebe wraps her arm around Janice's shoulder and gives her a little squeeze. 'No, no.' She can feel the tight ligaments beneath the soft fat. 'Unless you're looking for something different...' Phoebe is suddenly aware of a void of uncertainty before her and she becomes still with a distant expression.

Janice tweaks her neck to look at Phoebe's face. 'No, dear. I'm very happy with things just the way they are,' she lies.

Phoebe smiles and assists the old lady to the chair. She adjusts a smock around Janice's shoulders and leans forward conspiratorially. 'You are the very first customer to sit in this chair,' she whispers in her ear.

Janice's face lights up. 'Oh, I'm thrilled!'

Phoebe takes a quick glance out the window and, still with her mouth by Janice's ear, says absently, 'You will be.'

Janice surveys the mirror with a sardonic brow then looks away. She feels such a swelling of anguish, that she almost leaps out of the chair to escape it. But, Phoebe has taken that moment to recline the backrest, just as Janice lurches awkwardly.

'Oops... sorry, Janice. Are you okay?'

Janice lets herself subside.

Phoebe takes her hand and strokes it. 'Sorry,' she coos.

Janice remains still. She closes her eyes. A feeling of the past, welling to meet her, makes her feel a little nauseous. Most of her adult life, she has lived with the inkling of a vast dissatisfaction, never being able to even touch on its form and origin. And so, she has become preoccupied with the clamorous trivia of daily events, searching endlessly for the hidden sense in the gossip. Being elderly means having once been young, and Janice remembers perfectly well how she had felt—and what she had felt. But age and experience have not reconciled well, and just at this moment, she is ready to yield to any whim of the cosmos, if only it will precipitate sense from idle existence.

Phoebe prepares some dye at the bench and steals a look at her quiescent customer. Her gaze slides to the Thrum control at the junction of the seat and backrest. With held breath, Phoebe moves over and delicately flips the slot lever. She waits breathlessly for a response, but Janice remains inert. Then, with eyes wide, Phoebe presses a button to activate the pulse, and stands riveted, waiting for Janice to move.

Janice's eyes flick open. She raises her sight to Phoebe's alarmed face. 'I'm all right now, Phoebe.'

'Are you?' Phoebe chokes. 'That's good.'

Janice shifts in her chair and lets out a little groan.

Phoebe holds her breath. The noise from the street seems barely to reach them. A heavy silence settles. She has forgotten to switch on her cassette player. She bustles about with shampoo trays and hoses. Her hands are shaking as she guides the placid flow of the douche over Janice's hair. She works quietly, acutely aware of the annoying clarity of the falling water.

Janice clears her throat. 'Cassandra Prosser got engaged last week. Did you know?'

Slumping with relief, Phoebe gushes, 'Oh, yes. I did her hair.'

'The whole white wedding palaver it's going to be, too. There'll be more former boyfriends than relatives. It's scandalous. It makes a complete mockery of the institution of marriage, don't you think so, dear?'

'I know what you're...'

'And the shame of it is, that it will all end in divorce.'

'Yep—often does...'

'I always thought that she would marry young Jasper—you know, the Tomkins next door to me. I used to see those two having so much fun together when they were children. I suppose they became too familiar—do you think?'

'I couldn't say, Janice, I...'

'I think it was familiarity.'

Phoebe senses that a transformation is about to take place, but not in the way she was anticipating. She looks down at the Thrum controls then follows the lead from the chair to where it is plugged into an electrical socket hidden behind the bench corner. It looks switched on.

Janice sighs hugely. 'Oh, what does it matter. Familiarity is inevitable, especially after forty-eight years—how about that, Phoebe!'

'Forty-eight years!'

'Forty-eight years, Phoebe! Forty-eight years of eating chops—because you know, that is what he likes. He likes his chops, does Malcom—he likes his chops.' Janice squirms in her seat. 'Whoa... I don't know whether I'm feeling languorous or loquacious. Maybe a bit of both.'

Phoebe's hand slides to the controller. She makes a deft adjustment.

Janice continues, 'I suppose I should count myself lucky that he does most of the cooking now—all chops, mind! Him and his barbecue—chops, chops, chops. He wants to write a cookbook, you know—*Top Chops* or *Chips an' Chops* or *Chop Chop—Easy Meals for*

Carnivores, it doesn't really matter, he's just obsessed with cooking chops—chops, chops, chops... oh, my God!' Janice lifts her hands to her face and smothers a cry. Tears roll down her cheeks and onto her fingers.

Phoebe pulls a tissue from the box on the bench top and brushes it against Janice's cheek.

Janice pinches it between her fingers then scrunches it to her closed eyes. 'Oh Lordy, I don't know what's happening to me...'

Phoebe reaches down towards the Thrum control and makes another adjustment.

Janice nestles into the chair and separates her feet as far apart as possible on the foot rest. 'Just keep doing what you're doing, Phoebe dear. Don't mind me. I seem to be a bit restless today—a bit out of sorts— I'm not sure. Oh, I'm not sure what is going on.' She turns her head to the side. Her arms fall limp against the armrests and the tissue drops from her fingers.

Phoebe gently showers Janice's hair as she sleeps.

Kismet

Sunlight streams through the windows of the sunroom in Tiffany's house. She walks into the room holding two cups of tea.

Phoebe is plumped in the big arm chair with her legs over the armrests.

The change in her is an enormous relief to Tiffany; Phoebe is now effusive and alive with quirky mannerisms.

'It was fantastic, Tiff. She gave me a five-dollar tip. She loved it.' Phoebe paddles her feet with glee.

Tiffany listens and sips her tea, feeling a little buoyed with every swallow. She could never have imagined that Phoebe would embrace the Thrum chair quite to this extreme. She smiles when she recalls Phoebe's audacity.

The knock on her door late one evening came just as Tiffany was getting ready for bed. She padded out of her room and switched on the veranda light and was most surprised to see Phoebe's slight silhouette when she opened the door.

'Hi, Phoebe,' she said. 'Is everything okay?'

Phoebe rushed to reassure her that everything was fine, but that she had something that she was desperate to talk about, ever since the idea had popped into her head.

Tiffany pushed open the screen door and let Phoebe in. In the light of the hallway, Phoebe's face was suffused with excitement.

'Tiff,' she began, 'I've just come up with this idea, and I know it's going to sound crazy, but, well... you guys have started it, and I'm just taking it to the next level...'

For some reason, Tiffany knew what Phoebe was going to propose, and she couldn't help but clasp her hands over her mouth. Her words came out all muffled, 'Oh, my God!'

Phoebe knew then that she had made a terrible mistake—presuming that someone else might support her outlandish notion—and she too, clasped her hands to her mouth to stop herself from saying anything more.

The two of them stood in the hallway, boring into each other's eyes, each defying the other to commit to a spoken word.

At last, after enough time had passed for Phoebe to turn over a few other ideas to explain her late hour visit, her neighbour's eyes softened.

Tiffany's hands fell away so that just her fingers lingered on her lips. 'You want to put Thrum chairs in the Glamorama.'

Phoebe didn't know what to think anymore. She gave a tiny nod. Tiffany looked away with a frown and Phoebe's heart fell. What had she been thinking? It was totally preposterous—possibly even illegal. How could she have been so stupid! She backed up to the door and turned to open it. Then, she felt Tiffany's hand around her wrist. She stayed with her forehead against the flyscreen and tried to determine from the manner of Tiffany's grip whether she'd made a fool of herself.

At last she turned.

Tiffany was staring at her with a weird eagerness. 'Why not?' she said. Then she opened out her arms and said again, 'Why not?' She lunged at Phoebe and hugged her close and declared right next to her ear, 'Let's have a cuppa tea.'

They stayed up until the early hours, sipping tea and going over their conspiracy to create euphoria.

Tiffany sat hard up against the dining table, using her hands to accent her thoughts. '... it's not as though we have to have it on full-bore, so to speak.'

They giggled and wriggled self-consciously.

'It's hidden—and we'll introduce it very gradually.'

'Exactly! It's not going to be a case of, "Well, cop this, girls—this'll put you into orbit." No! We'll be, y'know—discreet... let it spread by word of mouth.'

Both burst out laughing.

Phoebe reached out to Tiffany's hand. 'Thanks, Tiff. You're such a friend. Now we just have to have this conversation with Ian.'

103

'... and Sonya.'

Tiffany looks at Phoebe over the rim of her teacup.

Phoebe makes big eyes at her. 'What?'

'Nothing—I was just thinking. How far did you go with Janice?'

'Hardly anything! I didn't want to, you know, overdo it. I just left it on broad—mild. Oh, look, she just loved it.' Phoebe gives a little bounce in the armchair. 'When she woke up, she insisted that I do more to her hair, so I sprayed in a pink, sort of band. She's two-tone now—mmm, nice tea, thanks.'

Tiffany looks away and smiles. 'Two-tone, huh. That's great, Phoebes. Well, can't undo what you've started.'

Phoebe laughs, 'What *we've* started!'

Tiffany puts down her cup then slaps her hands firmly onto her knees. 'Now,' she looks across to her new friend, 'stage two of the plan. Sonya is putting in a good word at the bowling club. Apparently, her game is hot, and the ladies literally want to know her secret. So, expect a few bookings there. She's also influential at the C.W.A. They're having a general meeting this week. Don't quite know what she's got in mind—something about redesigning the main street.' She absently reaches for her teacup. 'I can't believe I've lived next door to her for so long without knowing her any better.'

Phoebe smiles. 'Are you going to tell the girls at the roadhouse?'

'Yeah, but don't expect to see Miranda-the-dragon walking through your door any time soon—and tennis, there's a few girls there—and the school canteen... not a few frustrated mums whose lives could be changed, and anyone else I meet in the street.'

Phoebe swivels out of her seat, reaches across and clinks her teacup against Tiffany's. 'Thanks, Tiff.'

'Oh—guess what? Ian has finished the second chair.'

The two women stare goggle-eyed at each other for a moment then, together, they launch themselves from their chairs and rush for the hallway, screaming and laughing with cries of *me first!* echoing in the room before the door slams shut.

Still Reeling

The sword-wielding warrior is lit by weak streetlight. The sound of a Harley comes closer and its headlight pans across the steel door.

Max rides the bike up onto the footpath and lowers the stand, turning the handlebars so that the headlight shines full on the steadfast swordsman. He dismounts, painfully swinging his leg over the seat. With the engine still running, he walks tentatively to the entrance of his old haunt and unfastens a set of keys from his belt. He unlocks the padlock, slides open the bolt and swings open the door. His shadow looms long in the brick corridor. Max walks into the gloom, his riding boots scuffing now and again because of his awkward gait.

At the end of the corridor is another metal door that Max opens with the assistance of a carefully composed kick. He strokes the wall for the light switch. In the bleak fluorescent glare, he strides to a table in the middle of the room. On it is a cardboard box with an electrical lead dangling over the lip.

He leans with his knuckles on the table and spreads his feet a little. It's a sobering thought for him that the accumulations of three years in the town can fit into one cardboard box.

Still reeling from the encounter with Ian's chair and the subsequent fallout onto his life, Max's face is set with resentment, and revenge constantly occupies his mind.

He hefts the box to his chest, switches off the light and leaves without closing the door. Then he scuffs his way along the corridor into the yellow beam of the headlights. He rests his load on the Harley's saddle and, from a pannier, takes an elastic strap and secures the box against the sissy bar. Max walks back a few paces and kicks the steel door shut. The stern-faced warrior has a few more moments in the light before Max turns the bike around. He eases the bike off the kerb and onto the road. For a moment, the headlights light up the façade of the Glamorama across the street.

On an impulse, Max guns the motor, crosses the road and nudges the front wheel into the gutter so that the light shines through the display window. He slides off the bike and ambles across the footpath. Cupping his hands against the glass, he looks inside. The salon seems to smoulder in reflected beams.

We were a perfect and soulful match—but it was the wrong time.

Positioned above the mirrors, amongst the chrome and arcs of light, is a brilliant ink drawing, very large, of a Celtic warrior holding his princess. Both wear body adornments and both have tattoos of knots and swirls. She is wearing a neck torc of two entwined swans. At the bottom right hand corner, scrawled with flair, is the artist's signature—Max.

It pangs his heart to think that he and Phoebe will never share such a majestic union.

Rumour Mill

The wobbling black bowl establishes its centricity and rolls smoothly along over the clipped grass, headed with precisely gauged momentum for a soft collision with the cluster at the far end. Hearty applause issues from the white-clad women, huddled nearby.

Sonya has centre stage in this happy party. She is clearly dominating the popularity stakes here and she looks radiant, a fact that does not go unnoticed by her friends who all make occasional furtive glances in her direction. There is lots of chatter and laughter, and something Sonya says produces a particularly boisterous response, much to the annoyance of a group of male bowlers on the adjacent green.

The ladies make their way to the other end.

Maggie beseeches Sonya about her fabulous, forties-styled hair.

Jackie turns her sparrow face to look at Sonya with whimsical admiration.

The melee at the front of the school tuckshop almost overwhelms young Bryce, shuffling along in the queue, clutching his coins. His attention is not on the other children around him, but on Tiffany, happily dealing with lunch orders from the clamouring children. He can't take his eyes off her and follows her every movement, his mouth opening and closing in unselfconscious adoration.

The din seems to serve as a screen behind which the other mothers fearlessly eye Tiffany.

Then, as Bryce steps up to the counter, the children hush, in the universal way that children do when someone younger and cuter than they has the centre of attention. Heads still. Bryce holds out a fist full of coins and beholds Tiffany's lovely smile.

She leans over the counter and puts her face close by his. She takes Bryce's whole hand in hers.

Then, in a small, sharp voice, he says, *'You're beautiful!'* and the gush of laughter that follows is a natural affirmation of the truth.

Tiffany is delighted and pinches his cheek.

The other mothers chortle and smile and look with lingering envy in her direction.

It seems too early on a vibrant morning for conflict, but that is what humans create for themselves—only they call it sport. Over the years, the innocence of an impromptu football game played in bucolic tranquillity, has evolved into an earnest aspiration to win by all involved.

Phoebe, especially, played with an edgy single-mindedness that even the men in the team found slightly scary. But now, the implacable zeal has been replaced with an insouciance that amuses the other girls, but that infuriates Phil, the captain and the coach.

The play is at the other end of the field from where Phoebe and Jodee are in deep discussion. Both are wearing oversize BUTCHERS jerseys with their socks stretched and sagged under their shin guards.

Jodee focuses intently on something Phoebe is telling her. With startled eyes, her hands rush to cover her mouth.

At the far end of the field, things have taken a turn for the worse and the opposition is now in control. The horde thunders down the paddock. Phil bawls at the top of his lungs and the two women spring into action. But, to no avail. The goal is scored, and everyone walks solemnly back.

Phil berates Phoebe as he marches past.

Phoebe deftly falls in behind him and begins simulating a sexual grind. Players from both sides stifle their titters. Phoebe turns to a good-looking bloke from the opposition and says, 'I'll do this face to face with you, Fabian.'

He gives her an encouraging look.

The other girls eye Phoebe from under their brows.

Metamorphosis

The hairstyle is outlandish, and the make-up makes her look more like a victim than a celebrant of the feminine ideal. Despite the ambiance of glamour, the model appears wanton and dissolute and not at all infused with spirit and conviction.

Maggie, a lawn bowler, leans across to her neighbour on the couch, Lynne, a tuckshop mum, and proffers a look at the magazine photo. With doubtful shakes of the head, they point out to each other aspects they feel confident will receive reciprocal scorn.

Bettina, a soccer player from a nearby town, leans forward from where she is seated and has a critical look.

The three of them, now mutually assured of each other's stance on the latest fashions, lean back in their seats and resume reading.

Inside the Glamorama there is a restrained expectancy as the clients lounge with delicate poise. There are two Thrum chairs now. Phoebe attends to Jodee in one, while Tiffany briskly brushes the seat of the other chair and invites Maggie over. Lynne and Bettina stare steadily at their magazine and follow

Maggie's progress to the chair from the periphery of their vision.

Fidgeting with nerves, Maggie settles herself.

Tiffany lightly regales her with a story about the one and only time she played lawn bowls and how she had had the bias on the wrong side and, having launched the bowl with great composure, was mortified to see it skew across two other greens and end up in the gutter.

Everyone laughs, and Maggie relaxes.

Tiffany drapes her client and adjusts the Thrum control.

Phoebe flicks her a loaded glance as she attends to Jodee.

Jodee's eyes are closed and she is biting at her lip. Her head begins to roll—she looks pained, deliciously pained. Phoebe repositions her head and whispers for her to keep still.

The shuffling of shoes at the doorway attracts Phoebe's attention. Standing at the top of the stairs, wide-eyed and breathless, is Janice.

'Hello, Janice!' exclaims Phoebe with surprise, 'You're back soon. Perm holding alright, is it?'

The old lady blinks at the salon lights. 'Oh, yes dear, yes dear.' With a tight grip on the handrail, she says, 'I thought I might come for... something. What else do you do, Phoebe dear?'

Tiffany looks up. 'We can do a pedicure for you, Janice.'

Janice's eyes gravitate towards Phoebe's chair.

With slow emphasis Phoebe says, 'Janice... you'll

like it. I'm certain.'

Without a word, Janice moves towards the settee to await her turn.

Jodee always felt that it would be a betrayal to her sporty, boyish persona to disclose, completely, her femininity. Never convinced that females are entirely credible, she emerges onto the footpath outside the Glamorama feeling unreservedly sensual.

The few people that are about stop in their stride and have a good, long look at her.

She looks fantastic, dazzling, and she carries herself with confident aplomb. Jodee radiates joy in the most trivial of movements. She takes a deep breath, lifts her head and runs her tongue under her top lip in a small sensuous movement.

From up at the bakery, Iris straightens up from having made her latest blackboard update. It now reads just PIES—the SAUSAGE ROLLS having been freshly erased. She watches Jodee's swaying pelvis as she saunters up the footpath towards the bakery.

Maggie has rarely dared to entertain her voluptuous desires. Society's incessant programming has left her chronically anxious about the way she feels and the way she believes she should behave. The daring fantasies that she entertained whilst in the thrall of the chair, now seem outrageous and embarrassing.

She probes the last step onto the footpath and

steps into the sunlight, not fully believing that she has allowed this to happen to her. Phoebe has created a daring look for this senior citizen. She lifts her hands to her cheeks to feel the heat of her shame and turns, ready to go back inside. Then, she sees her reflection in the display window and halts. Maggie gazes, rapt. She has been transformed. Her hands travel from her face, down her breasts to her belly where they stay, pressing lightly.

An older gent passes by and bestows a lingering look.

Iris, mid-way through rubbing out PIES, looks hard as Maggie turns and strolls away.

Bettina has always been a strong individual and frequently felt the opprobrium that those, uninhibited enough, can expect from their peers in a small country town.

Dark and vivacious, she pitches out of the doorway to the Glamorama and props on the footpath. Bettina looks, and is, ready to mate. She adjusts the waistband of her underwear through her dress then stoops to peer into the cabin of a ute that is parked against the kerb.

Her husband, Nick, is asleep at the wheel.

With a gleam in her eye, visible even from the bakery, she strides to the passenger door, opens it wide and slides in. She settles herself close to her husband and brushes his face with her lips. She drops her hand below the steering wheel. Nick, his eyes wide, catapults forward and bangs his head on the sun visor.

Instinct

Iris retracts her head from the doorway of the bakery and leans against the jamb. She puts her fist to her mouth and takes a deep breath.

What she has seen in the past hour is inexplicable—totally inexplicable.

Like most shopkeepers, who regard the street and its passers-by with a predatory keenness, Iris is attuned, with neurotic intensity, to the tenor of life in the township. But, unlike most shopkeepers, she is not like that because of the needs of her business. In fact, the bakery is the cause of her gradual death, and there is nothing she dislikes more than having to cater for the population. Whenever Iris views the streetscape, she searches the faces for any abiding happiness, and the fact that she almost never encounters anyone deeply joyous, confirms to her that, like her, most people simply endure an existence.

Iris had never been able to prove herself in the way she wanted to, and she knows, deep down, that she will remain thwarted for the rest of her life. It would have helped if she had been able to put form to her desire, but her obsessions were always so elusive;

there were never the models and opportunities to inspire her in the little town; no one to help shape her hidden ideal—except doing French when she was at school.

And now, there are women leaving the hair salon who seem to be emanating something of great fulfilment, and Iris can't help but feel a shiver of portent.

She stares into space a while longer then, with a quick peek down the road, she steps onto the pavement, hefts the blackboard and carries it inside. Seconds later, she re-emerges without her apron. She brushes her dress with her hands, flicks back a few stray strands of hair, and marches down to the Glamorama.

The toenails are painted bright red and each one is separated from the other by a little foam disc. Tiffany applies lacquer with even strokes of the brush. She looks up as Iris walks into the salon. 'Hello, Iris. We won't be much longer—if you don't mind waiting a little while. Have a seat.'

Iris is riven with shock. She stares with barely disguised revulsion at Janice, reclining in the canted chair, with her knees slightly out and her feet resting on fold-out extensions. Janice's breathing is surprisingly rapid considering the languor of her situation, and Iris can see in the mirror that, every now and again, her eyelids tremble open to reveal nothing but white underneath.

In the other seat, Lynne arches her neck and

lurches away from the backrest. Phoebe quickly takes her shoulders and gently repositions her. Lynne licks her lips and rolls her head from side to side.

Phoebe smiles urgently at Iris as she fiddles with something beside the seat.

Lynne opens her mouth—she strains and reddens. Her eyes flick open—she can't breathe.

Phoebe focuses on a spot at the juncture of the seat and backrest and manipulates something out of Iris's sight.

Tiffany comes over and mutely stands by with her brush poised in mid-air.

Lynne's body goes rigid and her eyes begin to rotate upwards. She catches sight of something above the mirrors. Her eyes widen; she is being saved—saved by a Gallic warrior with tattooed swirls on his muscular arms. The pent blood pulses at her temples and a rapturous smile lights her face. Her eyelids flutter and she falls backwards against the chair in a dead faint.

Phoebe looks across at Tiffany.

They both steal a glance at Iris.

With a slack mouth, Iris stares at the unconscious Lynne.

Phoebe reaches over to the dressing table and picks up a palette and a soft brush. She commences brushing rouge onto Lynne's now ashen cheeks. She smiles and mouths, 'She won't be long.'

Iris nods. She backs up to a seat. Having cocooned desires of her own for so long, she finds it difficult to accept that other women seek greater glories. To see Janice disported in the recliner chair in such an abandoned way, and to see Lynne in a wanton swoon, comes as unexpectedly as the mad joy that clutches at her chest.

Time Without End

The original building at the back of the bakery, long disused and so full of dusty junk that it is almost unnavigable, contains a large brick oven. The arched mouth of the oven has been bricked up, and all around it are hornet nests and spider webs. Across the room from the oven, and up a short flight of stairs, is the door that leads to the front of the shop. Iris is standing in the opening, gazing at the place that she has for so long been trying to forget.

She has been transformed. Her hair is a bouncy body of loose curls shaped with a slanted bob, and her make-up highlights the beauty that is not always visible in her face.

The experience at the Glamorama, in the thrall of the chair, had been overwhelming. For an eternal moment, the Earth really had stood still for her.

Iris had returned to the bakery heady and expansive and had closed the shop early—not that anyone noticed. Then she'd gone to the back of the shop and, for the first time in many years, turned the big key in the old door. She reefed it open and stood aside as the dust cascaded to the floor. When the air cleared, she stepped out onto the landing above the stairs and tried to remember the young woman, already divorced, who had hidden her hopes and dreams in a bricked-up crypt.

She descends the stairs, her eyes never straying from the brick arch. Gripped in her right hand is a large knife. When she is in front of the oven, she raises it and begins to gouge at the soft mortar. She prises out the bricks with her strong hands. Gradually, she dismantles the wall. A pile of rubble grows at her feet. Soon the oven opening is cleared. Deep inside the black cavern there is a large metal flour tin. Iris steps over the rubble and reaches in. With an effort, she slides the tin out. Placing it in a clear space on the floor, she levers off the lid. Inside the tin are magazines that she reverently pulls out and places onto the old kneading bench. They are fashion magazines, and they are all in French.

Iris takes one of the magazines and kneels on the dusty floor. She thumbs through it on her lap. Her eyes rest on a photo of a model revealing a cossetted bosom. Her hand runs down her neck to the buttons of her dress. Absentmindedly, she undoes the top few and, folding the rims, she creates a V collar that plunges deep into the flesh of her breasts.

Life In Parallel

Ian adds a packet of upholsterer's tacks to a small plastic tray overflowing with a metal melange of hardware. Deep in thought, he makes his way between the aisles.

Ellen follows his progress beneath a haughty brow. The only way that she can prevent her emotions from pulling at her face is by affecting a superior condescension. But, her expression softens as she notes Ian's dilemma—at not being able to find anything that he needs. She gives a little inward laugh. *This has been going on for so long*.

Ian's visits to the hardware over the last few years have been more touching for Ellen than she could ever have believed. He always arrived at about eleven—the morning rush of tradesmen would have dissipated by then and the shop was often empty until lunchtime. She would watch him as he idled among the shelves and wonder what game he was playing at. She knew it was a game—one that she did not discourage, but one in which she was uncertain of her role. She felt comforted by his presence, yet most times there was only the barest verbal exchange between them—on many occasions not even a single word—even after he had spread his collection of parts onto the counter and had waited for her to tally the amount and book it to his account. Not a word. Just a look—a cheeky grin from him—to which she invariably held up a derisive countenance. To have said anything at all, especially something as prosaic as 'thank you' would have been a travesty.

But today is different; today Ian seems to emanate an assurance that she has never noticed before and, as he arrives at the counter, Ellen positions herself in between him and the halo of glare from the street and says, 'Ian, I must confess, this time I really am curious.'

'Oh.' Ian pretends to be crushed. 'I thought you were always curious, but just didn't say so in order to deny me the pleasure of telling you.'

Ellen eyes him obliquely and gathers in the tray. 'We had a C.W.A. meeting last night. Sonya has taken charge. Everyone supports her. She's talking about a cake stall at the market next month to raise money for the Butchers. I know they haven't won a game all year, but Sonya thinks new jerseys will make all the difference. She's started a ballot for a name change too."

Ian's eyes narrow with the effort of concentrating.

'We're also thinking of helping Janice and Malcom to publish a cookbook. It's all very invigorating, but not at all like the old Sonya. I'm sure that you have something to do with it, Ian. Coincidences, perhaps? I don't think so. That's why I really am curious.' Ellen gives a lopsided pout. 'And I don't pretend not to be interested to deny you a chance to tell me.' She bites at the corner of her lip. 'I pretend not to be interested so that I don't have to hear.'

'Really, Ellen—you don't want to hear?'

'It's terrible of me. I don't want to hear, because I'm envious of you.'

Ian winces. 'What?'

Ellen wants to confess, but is finding it difficult to look Ian in the eye. 'You do what you're good at—you always have, even when we were at school.'

To give Ellen some emotional room, Ian looks away. 'Well, I didn't know any better. There's always one in the crowd.' He laughs.

Ellen seems mesmerized and stares out into the shop. 'I stopped doing what I was good at...'

'Do you remember what you were good at, Ellen? Do you remember the time the two of us went in your dad's car to the lookout and, instead of doing a portrait of me like you were supposed to, you got out all your paints and painted a prang on the side of the car—with twisted metal and shattered glass, and a gash in the door that you could see the seats through. It looked like it had been set upon by a giant can opener. I was laughing my head off, driving home, through town, and everybody gawking and pointing. It was brilliant!'

'And we parked the car in front of the house where Dad could see it.'

Ian is rocking with laughter. 'I thought we were dead for certs when he came out. Like a bloody zombie he was, staggering across the lawn to the car—and his face, a couple of feet from ours—until he realised it was paint. Oh shit, you were shaking. I was shaking—he thought his car was wrecked...' Ian freezes and looks oddly stricken.

Ellen squares up to him looking fiercely alive. The profile that she mostly keeps hidden, in her manner and with the assistance of the stark contrast of inside and outside light, is now visible—the scars, red and livid with emotion, that come so close to her eye and pull at the features on that side of her face. 'It was prophetic, wasn't it? Dad only had the car a few more months after that. And I still have my paints... and I've never used them.' Ellen bows her head and sobs.

Ian looks around. They are alone. Ron must be out the back at the trade drive-through. When he turns, Ellen is suddenly there right in front of him, reaching for his shoulders and dropping her head onto his chest. He looks down at her hair and remembers it being the same as it was when they had cuddled in the bus on the way back from a school excursion. He enfolds her in his arms and feels the unfamiliar contours of her body through her dress.

Ellen scrunches the front of Ian's shirt, nestles in closer under his chin, and gives a long, shuddering sigh.

Outside, the street is quiet, just as things always were for Ian when Ellen was near. As teenagers, there had been the vitality of youthful obsession that imbued everything that happened around them, and they had been caught up in the innocent wonderment of each other. It had been playful and reciprocal; it was the budding of their erotic nature. Then, abruptly, it had ended, and for a while, until he met Sonya, Ian ached for the friendship that was no longer possible.

When he was away at tech-college, Ellen and Ron had expediently married. Ian was genuinely happy for them both. The whole town was happy for them. Then, he had been whisked away with his work, and thoughts of Ellen surfaced only on the rare occasions when he'd go to the hardware. Those times were difficult encounters. He would do his best to deal only with Ron. Whenever he did see Ellen, he felt so overwhelmed that he couldn't think straight, and would leave believing that he'd upset her. He would agonize over the past, the present and what could be.

Over time, the fulfilment of both their lives made it easier for them to reconcile the past, and yet, with such vivid memories of the picnic table, Ian always hoped to restore something of the burgeoning sensual adventure that they had enjoyed—to achieve nothing more than to affirm what they had shared.

And then, he had retired early. His projects at home required more frequent visits to the hardware. One day, he stood at the foot of the steps and came to the sudden conclusion that it was important to see Ellen again. He trotted up and smiled at her from behind a display stand. He couldn't think of anything to say, so he didn't. Instead, he perused the aisles and idly collected bits and pieces that would be useful to him. He'd been doing this, about once a week, for years now; his house had every hook, latch and handle conceivable.

Thus, in his quiet way, he cultivated an erotic interplay that, despite its awkwardness, he knew was helping to mend something in Ellen. Even though she remained aloof, it was all part of giving her the chance to change—one day—in some way.

As he brushes his hand over Ellen's bra strap, he knows that he would never want to have a sexual liaison with her, nor she with him. It was not about sex; it was about eroticism. She started it after all—coercing him to pose starkers!

Ian draws himself straight and comforts the nape of Ellen's neck as he peers out through the display window.

Across the road, Iris straightens up from her pavement board and considers it. She turns and faces the street for a view at her world. She looks different. Iris is wearing deep red lipstick and her attire is a unique marriage of ingénue and French Madame.

A man passes by and has a jolly good look at Iris's magnificently displayed décolletage. She turns and goes inside. The man reappears, has a quick look at the blackboard and follows Iris into the bakery. On the blackboard is written, in lovely copperplate script: *Vol-au-vents, quiche Lorraine, mini-soufflés, croissants, coquettes.*

A Rolls-Royce idles past. Moira pulls herself up against the steering wheel and peers into the bakery.

A little noise issues from inside the hardware.

Ian turns his head.

Ron is poised at the end of an aisle, a marker pen half raised in the air. 'Everything alright, Ian?'

Ian nods and gives a little thumbs-up from behind Ellen's back.

Ron harks back his head, a quizzical smile on his lips. Then, with an emphatic nod, he slips the marker back in his apron and makes his way to the back of the shop.

Ellen puts her hands up to Ian's shoulders and separates from him. 'Sorry, Ian,' She retrieves a handkerchief from her sleeve and blows her nose.

Ian gives her one last little squeeze on her waist. 'That's okay, Ellen.'

Ellen dabs her eyes and composes herself with a large breath, 'Do you know what else Sonya is organizing?'

Ian shakes his head.

'She's organizing a dance... where *I* will have as much of a chance as anyone of being the belle of the ball.' She draws an elegant hand along the scars of her smiling face.

Ian looks down at her with a patronizing smirk.

Ellen slants a grin at him, 'It's going to be a masked ball!'

They burst out laughing, clutching each other with glee.

Ian pulls Ellen close and holds her under his chin. He scans the distance across the street.

Iris is standing on the footpath in front of the

bakery, in animated conversation with her gentleman customer, he clutching a white paper bag. They flirt amiably then bid each other a cheery farewell.

Purple

Lost in thought, Iris dwells for a moment with a grin on her lips. So much loveliness has been restored to her face just through her changing her mind.

And, how about that! The first bloke that walked by, had asked about her coquettes and she had delivered. Lifting her brow as she sidled up to him from behind the counter, running her finger down his chest and pressing her bosom to his elbow, she'd said, 'If you like my coquette, you'll love my croquettes...'

They both had a good laugh. He said he was from out of town, but he promised her that he'd return.

She blinks at the sunlight and is about to move off the footpath, when she wavers and stills. With a few sliding steps, she moves out towards the kerb and contemplates the building next door—the quixotic Empire Fashion House. Bidden by a nascent urge, she walks towards the arched display window and gazes into it. Her reflection superimposes over the exhibited articles. She is not looking at anything in particular— rather, she is spellbound by the idea of it all. But, the look of wonderment transforms to a brow fraught with doubt.

Iris had become profoundly depressed by the loss of her dreams so long ago, and when Moira filled the window next door with such an overt spectacle of fashion extravaganza, it twisted Iris into the harridan that everyone has come to know. Whilst she felt envious of Moira's accomplished savoir-faire, and bitter about her own predicament, she reserved the greatest hostility for the passers-by who were unable to acknowledge the culture and haute-couture so flamboyantly presented right next door.

And so, poor Iris baked her pies and sausage rolls, wetting the dough sometimes with her own tears, obsessed in a paradox of emotions, never realising how close she was to redemption all along.

A look of defeat rests on Iris's face—though it is impossible to tell whether it is from a lack of courage, or because of the hideously expensive price tags on the apparel.

One thing does catch her eye—a corset in lurid purple.

Iris looks to the stone portal and walks towards it.

Moira's gloved hands tremble as she places a record on the gramophone. She gives a few measured turns of the winder and flicks the lever. The strains of Verdi's 'Ritorna Vincitor' from Aida crackles from the horn.

The gramophone had belonged to Moira's grandfather and its dulcet trumpeting was the first indicator to her that there was another world beyond the fences and the cattle crushes. Fairy tales and history books all ran together, but the sound of opera was living proof of a more exalted stage, and from then on, Moira devoted herself to becoming a diva.

Leaving for the city, she acquired an eccentricity and hedonism that surpassed even that of her contemporaries, at a time when overindulgence was the cultural idiom. Frustratingly, her forays abroad coincided with the war, and her career as a singer stalled. Then, the musical styles changed. When she tried to reinvent herself, she found that her voice was ruined from smoking. A life of pleasure and loving seemed precipitously doomed, and in a grandiose show of defiance, she bought a Rolls-Royce. Then, when the Gatton dynasty disintegrated, she was left with an ultimatum—live in the family mansion or lose it. To her intense chagrin, this development actually suited her; her lifestyle was untenable, her prospects bleak. So, in a last hurrah, she filled her apartment to overflowing with posh, arty acquaintances and bade them all a fond adieu. She mumbled something about family commitment and the call of duty, which impressed her friends into outpourings of commiseration and awe. Then, she made the long trip from Melbourne to oblivion.

Unfortunately for Moira, her lifestyle was chronically extravagant, and so an offer to teach French at the high school was loftily accepted. The Empire Fashion House was Moira's retreat from the stultifying tedium of country living. Here she displayed the jewels from another era, and as long as she paid the rates, she could flaunt to her heart's content and no one would mind, nor, in time, care. That was when the palsy began.

And now, for the first time, someone has walked through the entrance portal with the look of want on her face, and for Moira, the triumph is complete.

There are shelves of decorative objects and racks of dark garments in the gloom of the emporium. Nearby is a cheval mirror and reflected in it is Iris's naked torso. Moira's gloved hands come from behind and cup Iris's breasts. She hefts them lightly, her palsy causing Iris's breasts to ripple.

Moira's gaunt face appears over Iris's shoulder and she turns to her ear. Her voice is hoarse. She speaks to Iris in French.

'Iris, you have done this before—you do it every day—it should not be unfamiliar to you.'

Iris responds in schoolgirl French, '... *je fais, Madame?*'

'Yes. You begin with the dough—it is cold and lifeless, but your hands warm it—and the warmth gives life. You can feel it swelling.' Moira lifts Iris's breasts a little higher. 'Do you feel it?'

Iris closes her eyes to better concentrate on her French. '... *oui, Madame... je peux le sentir...*'

'*Bon, bon*—and it keeps on rising.' She lifts Iris's breasts higher. 'And what must you do then?'

Iris struggles for the correct words. '... *je l'ai mis... leur...*'

'You put them in the tins, yes?'

134

'*Oui, Madame*. They rise in the tins.'

From the side, Moira's young assistant, an after-school French student, produces the purple corset and positions it against Iris. Moira lifts Iris's breasts high and the assistant slides the corset up and underneath. The old lady then delicately lowers Iris into the cups.

The purple satin shimmers dully. Iris gasps as Moira pulls at the laces.

'Now, you hope,' Moira strains with effort, 'that everything will go well. It is your creative purpose, yes? —to sustain life, to nurture.' She deftly ties a bow and turns Iris around. Her 'buns' have risen; the corset has given Iris a most compelling décolletage. Moira chortles deeply, 'Iris, you are magnificent. Now it is time to go on display.' She dusts a little talc over Iris's bosom and brushes it lightly.

Iris admires herself in the mirror and whispers, 'At last... I can love myself.'

Moira croons, 'You won't be the only one.'

Courage

What makes Iris feel so delightfully kindled the next day, as she sips from a translucent china tea cup, is the spark of her elemental erotic nature.

Moira knows this all too well; one doesn't live in the art world without coming to understand the relationship of eroticism to performing; the consummate performer becoming one with the receptive audience in a cycle of exhibitionism and adulation, morphing into erogenous hysteria. Of course, this is just tea between friends, but to both, after so long an arid period, it is opening night, and each fulfils the other's needs in a fine interplay of life's essential drama—the quest for survival.

The cake plate with its scattering of crumbs is cleared away by Moira's assistant. She returns with a new pot of tea and places it amidst the exquisite little table set.

Moira is at ease here, in her bohemian retreat. She draws luxuriantly on her filter and poses, oblivious of her quiver. 'Quite simply, delicious, Iris. I'm so relieved. The food in this town has never excelled. What a surprise you are. We must do this regularly.'

'*Merci, Madame.*' Iris has never before in her life felt

so stirred; the echoes of the classroom come to her as though she was at her desk. She seizes words that she hasn't heard for forty years. *'Ce serait... dommage... de ne jamais avoir excellé... après tout ce temps.'*

Moira nods with a pointed look. 'It would, indeed, be a shame to never have excelled after all this time.'

Iris holds out her hand over the table. She is holding a thin wad of hundred-dollar notes.

Moira's hand hovers over the money. 'I will take just one of these, my darling.' She lifts off one note.

'But, that is not the price.' Iris says in astonishment.

'Ah, the prices, my dear,' Moira drawls, 'are there to frighten away the timid. But you? —you will never be frightened again, I can see that. Now, you must go and feed the masses.' She surveys Iris's bosom through a cloud of smoke.

Feel the Difference

Now, whilst it's well and good to consider the higher forms of human existence, there's nothing quite as life-affirming as a really good root, and Lynne and her husband are making the most of a tricky situation, given that their children's demands are almost as primal as theirs.

With her pretty face framed by the cluster of tight curls of a twenties-style bob, she leans out of her bedroom window and watches as her children dart in and out of their newly built cardboard cubby house. The curtains, tightly drawn across Lynne's back, billow and fold strangely. She responds to the children's strident calls, 'Yes, I can see you! You're all very good. Very good.' She rocks backwards and forwards rhythmically. The curtains bulge and crease. Again, she calls out with surprising urgency, 'Yes, you're good. Very good!'

She lowers her head to the sill and whimpers, 'Oh, so good. Oh, so good...' as the curtains waft in time with her movements.

Janice emerges from the kitchen into the dining room. She is holding a large plate of chops, beautifully presented with steaming vegetables and garnished with an eggplant and mushroom sauce. Her hair is a peacock blue with a candy pink in the undercut. She's wearing a generously proportioned apron that goes to just above her knees, and she approaches her husband with a glimmer of pride on her lovely smile.

Malcom beholds her with adoration, searching her face in abject worship as she puts down the plate in front of him. She plants a kiss on his forehead.

Janice sets her hands on her back, and the bright red lacquered nails of her fingers dig little dimples into the white skin of her completely bare bottom.

New Perspectives

Ian rolls the trolley out from under the roller door towards the road verge where his car and trailer are parked. He balances a pink Thrum chair with one hand and steers up to the tail gate. There is another Thrum chair, lime, already tied down in the front of the trailer. With an effort, he levers the chair into place and commences tying it down.

The afternoon sun glows just above the houses. A car comes around the corner. It slows down and stops against the gutter. Phoebe gets out and walks towards Ian. She runs her hand over one of the chairs. 'Hi, Ian.'

'Hello, Phoebe.'

They lean against the chairs and look at each other with suppressed mirth.

Phoebe holds her hands to her face. 'I can't believe we're doing this!'

With a level eye, Ian replies solemnly, 'It's making a difference—to a lot of people.'

Phoebe peeks through her fingers. 'Yes, it is.'

A currawong hops across the grass nearby in search of its last meal for the day.

Ian looks at the ground. 'How's Max?'

Phoebe leans back and clutches the tie rail. 'I know where he is—but, I haven't contacted him.' She tilts her head towards Ian and draws a coy pout. 'He's not really a bikie, you know.'

Ian snorts. 'Well, perhaps not. But he did threaten to kill me.'

'He won't,' Phoebe says, squinting against the setting sun. 'He really is... he is actually very sensitive.' She frowns. 'I mean, he's been looking, you know, for somewhere to fit in. The whole bikie thing—it was an experiment, to acquire an identity. Oh, I know it all sounds corny, Ian. We all do it. Except you.' Phoebe laughs.

She has a deep, unfettered laugh that Ian knows comes from someone who understands the value of love. And now, as they share this rare intimacy, Ian can't help but feel the greatest affection for a woman, so vulnerable and so strong.

'Why are you staring at me like that, Ian?'

He comically rolls his eyes. 'It's nothing.'

'See, you have your interests. Your glass is always half full, isn't it?'

Ian stares into the distance. 'Completely full, Phoebe—though it's just a small glass.'

The radiance of the autumn afternoon makes everything around them glow deeply, and in a moment of ethereal clarity, Ian understands that, just as the sun can change the day simply by shining from a different angle, people can change by looking at life from a new perspective.

'How are we going to fill Max's glass, Phoebe? I had no idea that he was so interested in Celtic art. I couldn't help noticing the drawings in your lounge—you know... after Max had his accident.'

Phoebe's whole body is cast in a golden light as the sun makes one last appearance between the houses. 'Are you interested in the Celts, Ian?'

'All ancient civilizations, actually.'

'Wow! You share an interest with Max.' Phoebe hugs herself. She slides over to Ian and leans against him. 'See, Max is upset with life because we don't make beautiful things any more—no stone buildings, no monuments, no fine craftwork, artworks. No wisdom— the knowledge of the ancients has evaporated. He thinks that only truly civilized people would be capable of such beauty. He can't explain the wars and the horror, except to say that it takes ages to achieve beauty, and only hours to destroy it. His tattoos are, as he says, a paradox; he has mutilated his body with the most exquisite art. You should have a look at them sometime.'

The sun has gone down, and everything has become grey, including the pallor of Ian's face. He puts his arm around Phoebe.

Phoebe opens the door into the drab lounge. The weak twilight that filters in through the blinds is all she wants as she makes her way to the telephone. She taps in a number and waits for the connection to be made.

On the wall above her, a flaxen-haired giant holds

his princess in a peremptory embrace, challenging the onlooker with fearless, gimlet eyes. And she, half turned with an open hand over his broad, tattooed chest, looks out over his sinewy arm with doe-like wonder.

Phoebe's eye travels down to the delicate signature. A tear rolls to the corner of her mouth. The connection is made. 'Max?'

The line remains silent.

'Max... I need you. There's work for you... doing body art. There's a demand for it now. We're going to be alright. I want to see you again.'

She puts down the phone.

Luckily for Phoebe, in a time of great torment, when she had said and done things that were out of character, she had three good neighbours to help her. For much of the time with Max, Phoebe was surrounded with conflicts, but no matter what anyone said about him, she could always see the trailing glory—his art, his insight—and his devotion.

And now, at last, it is the time for them to be together, to create that synthesis of art and adornment—the body beautiful.

The reflection of the road seems endless in Max's mirror shades. The wind whips at his jacket and his helmet glints with sunlight. He pushes the Harley-Davidson through a sweeping bend. The growl of the motor is not yet embarrassing to Max; for the moment it is still the most satisfying way to express his inner rage. As he bullets along on a country morning, he is very much in control—the irony, of course, being that he can only go where the road takes him.

The bike roars up a rise and gradually disappears behind the crest, the image shimmering in the heat before it vanishes in the azure sky.

The air is quiet again and the eternal blue prevails.

Moira Gatton's ravaged visage lifts to the sun. The unrelenting light savages the thick and broken make-up on Moira's hawkish face as she serenely pans the road, listening to the diminishing echoes of the Harley's exhaust.

Her clothes are fabulous. Despite the sunny day, she is wearing a full-length Schiaparelli coat in hyacinth blue, and offsetting the masculine profile, it is teamed with a slim, grey accordion-pleated skirt with patent leather belt and tortoiseshell clasp. Her cream blouse is double layered silk chiffon and the loosely choked cravat matches the deep blue of the coat lining. She stands in the gravel by the side of the road in medium high opera pumps that crunch as she turns to meet Ian who is walking up to her.

'Just a loose connection, Moira.' Ian squints and smiles.

They face each other, Moira slightly taller.

Ian wipes his hands and harks his head towards the Rolls, parked awkwardly in the road siding. 'A beautiful car.'

Moira composes herself and replies in well-modulated tones, 'Yes, indeed. It came as an unpleasant surprise though, when it stopped motoring. Most unpleasant, Ian—particularly in view of the isolation.' From her coat she withdraws a slim, beautifully crafted wallet, and with her gloved hands shaking uncontrollably, she attempts to open it. 'I'm very grateful for your timely arrival, Ian Shaw. I must compensate you for the repairs to my vehicle. I do appreciate it awfully.'

Ian steps closer and cups his hands around Moira's. 'It's my great pleasure, Moira. Truly.'

The old woman rears a little at this unexpected intimacy, but Ian, still with his hands over hers, leans even closer to her and speaks to her ear while she surveys the horizon.

Ian withdraws and appeals to Moira with a raised brow and steepled fingers.

Moira's eyes narrow. A hideous, conspiratorial grin materializes on her face. She chortles, 'I believe I shall, Ian. I believe I shall.'

Ian averts his sight. 'I'll get the car started for you.' He turns and crunches back to the Rolls.

Moira looks after him and ponders what it is that has changed in her town. Having lived for long enough to know that nothing in life is accidental—such as the Rolls breaking down in the middle of nowhere— she grins with wrinkled perspicacity at Ian's tit-bit of information—that she should visit the Glamorama.

Satisfied Customers

For Ian, filling up at the roadhouse has always been an uncomfortable confirmation of civilization being out of sync with the cosmos. But, now there are little touches to show that people are welcome, and as the trucks roll out and the palls of diesel smoke add to the certainty of our eventual annihilation, Ian smiles at the grim pathos—that failing helps us to live, but that not trying is certain death.

He returns the nozzle to the bowser and walks to the entrance of the roadhouse. Inside, a number of truck drivers are sitting at the tables with their meals in front of them. Whereas previously the meals were anything but inspired, now there are garnishes, side salads, browned pastries as well as sauces, gravy decanters and bottles of salad dressing.

Angela is sitting on the knee of one of the drivers, chatting and laughing with the group. Her hair is a flagrantly come-hither pile of loose curls and abandoned wisps and licks.

She spies Ian. 'Ian! Hang on.' She leaps off the man's knee and rushes to him, electric, flustered and gushing, and just the sort of restorative Ian needs to know that what is happening inside the Glamorama is definitely in tune with Mother Nature.

'I'm starting at Phoebe's tomorrow, Ian. I'm sorry it's such short notice.'

'Oh, that's alright,' he replies with a dismissive wave. 'I'm sure Sonya will cope until the new girl starts.'

'Thanks.' Angela looks uncertain about something.

Ian reassures her, 'Don't worry about it—she's happy to help out.'

Angela moves close to Ian. 'Oh, I know—she'll be fine here...' she lowers her voice, 'and Miranda,' she looks about, 'is really, you know, quite sweet now that...' she faces Ian squarely, 'she's had her hair done.'

Ian nods infinitesimally and wonders what he has created.

A fat lock of hair falls across Miranda's working brow. Her chin presses against the tomato red vinyl of the Thrum chair, this model deployable as a massage/tattoo table, with the Thrum apparatus positioned to give alternative experiences for the clients. She is lying front down with her face to the side, her eyes now turning to Claire, also front down on her table and facing Miranda, an arm's-length away.

Now and again, Miranda squeezes shut her eyes and licks her lips. She adjusts the sonic pulse to spread over her favourite part, and the ballistic surge to orgasm holds her suspended for long enough to make it scintillatingly clear to her that love exists beyond any norms. No longer will she be scornful of sex—

that complex miasma of being gorgeous and sexually charged—and being contemptuous of her lovers. In the past she had allowed sex to dominate, and gradually relationships with men became detestable to her.

On the neighbouring table, Claire makes some unusual noises, audible over the music which, nowadays, is turned up pretty loud.

Miranda reassures her with an indulgent wink then closes her eyes again. This is a pleasure she has dreamed about; a pleasure that has fulfilled her expectations; a pleasure she always knew was attainable— if only...

Miranda's skirt is bunched around her waist, and her red underpants are pulled down far enough so that Max can work freely on her upper buttock. His forearm rests on Miranda's bottom as he ever so carefully executes delicate lines with the tattoo pen. Resting in the small of Miranda's back is the material from a torn pocket with the embroidered logo of a flying swift. Max's pen unerringly traces its course over Miranda's skin, slowly recreating the stylized bird.

Miranda doesn't flinch. Her trailing arm moves sideways a little to allow her hand to drop to the control panel. She makes some adjustments and is about to relax again when she sees Claire, with wide-eyed urgency, beginning to pant. Miranda reaches out and brushes Claire's cheek.

Claire grasps Miranda's fingers then, gasping, she presses the back of Miranda's hand to her lips to stifle her cry as she experiences an orgasm for the first time.

They remain connected until Miranda retrieves

her hand. Then she places her fingers against her own mouth and shudders with her own climax.

Max, quite indifferently, lifts his pen. Leaving a hand on Miranda's bottom in order to preserve contact, he uses the moment to rearrange some equipment. He unscrews his water bottle one-handed and takes a swig.

Miranda's arm falls limp. Max reaches down and lays it alongside her. Then he switches off all the dials on the Thrum panel and resumes tattooing, his head bent low over Miranda's white flesh.

This is no longer a revelation to Max—not that it is no longer a mystery; it's just that he has seen it happen a number of times now and the result is always the same—a satisfied customer who leaves the salon with a new view of the world.

Beside him, Angela has positioned Claire comfortably and turned the Thrum dials to an idle setting. She peels the stencils from Claire's shoulder and puts away the pots of henna.

Claire stares into the distance. Something in the knowing arch of her eye foretells of fewer dropped sausages and far more satisfying customer relations.

Angela puts another incense stick into the holder and holds a lighter to it. Through the spiralling smoke she looks over at Tiffany. They exchange a secret smile.

Tiffany is attending to one of the bowling ladies, Jackie, a diminutive, bird-like woman with a look of surprise bordering on alarm. She squirms as though something is not right, lifting her brows repeatedly over her round eyes.

Tiffany speaks softly into her ear and guides the woman's hand to the dials. Her tiny fingers fret at the controls.

Reaching behind her for the hair dryer, Tiffany switches it on and waves it aimlessly about near her client. The little woman is looking like a surprised owl about to 'hoo hoo', and if she should, it would be barely audible above the noise of the dryer.

Tiffany scans the long wall mirror. Everyone is absorbed—the hairdressers in their clients, and the clients in themselves.

There are six chairs in the salon now, and Denise, from the other salon, is working for Phoebe.

Phoebe walks from the coat stand near the entrance (another of Ian's resurrected inventions) to the counter, holding out a long black coat into which she assists Moira.

Moira's hair is... no different than usual really; her hair has always been rather well presented, in a style that she has retained since the war—the Second World War, not the First.

Phoebe goes to the other side of the counter.

Moira reaches into the coat pocket and pulls out her wallet, in the process catching a glimpse of herself in the mirror. She steps sideways to get an unobstructed view and frames her face with her hands. She is statuesque.

Phoebe holds her breath.

Moira has been transformed; she is the Duchess of

Windsor; she is Marlene Dietrich—Greta Garbo. She is the embodiment of an ideal— not actual, yet not an illusion.

Moira examines her reflection for a moment longer. Then, she neatly plucks a hundred dollar note from her wallet and proffers it across the counter. Her hand is as steady as a rock.

Phoebe takes the note and gets the change out of the till.

Moira protests at Phoebe's outstretched hand. 'Keep the change, dahling. That was wonderful— simply wonderful. Please see that I have a regular booking... let's say, once a week.'

Phoebe riffles through the appointment book. 'Thank you, Ms Gatton. Shall we make it a week from today... ten-ish?'

'That will do nicely.' With an afterthought, she purrs, 'and please accept this.' She withdraws from her pocket an ebony cigarette holder. She holds it out without a quiver. 'I won't need this now. It's a Beech-Harrison, you know—but one can become too eccentric. It may make an interesting display—subject of conversation...'

All the while she has been admiring herself. 'Good day.'

Phoebe assists Moira down the stairs and out onto the footpath where her Rolls is parked with one wheel up on the kerb and with an envelope tucked behind the wiper blade.

With an imperious wave of her hand, Moira

indicates that Phoebe should take the envelope and throw it away.

True Art

It is the end of the day, and the street is deserted. Max is sprawled in one of the salon's lounge chairs with a sketchbook on his lap. He looks out through the display window at the greying buildings opposite and has a quiet chuckle at the newly painted artwork surrounding *Sally's Mustering Yard*, the recently opened saddlery. Above the veranda are sheet-steel sculptures of rearing horses and whip-cracking riders. Next door, the veterinarian's practice has a long mural along the façade of the most gorgeous animals cavorting, rolling, flying, gambolling and slithering, all in a frenzy of playful encounter.

Between these two buildings is a steel door that leads to the premises behind. Max's stare is intense. Painted on the door is a garden gate, complete with an arbour of miniature roses. On the painted gate is a painted shingle on which is written in fine cursive script: *Arbour Amore—for Lovers of the Garden*. It is the place of his former hell.

He takes a reflective swig of his beer and puts the bottle back down at his feet. He smooths the page of his sketchpad with a sweep of his hand and, glancing intermittently at a book of ancient art lying open beside him, resumes sketching one of the photographs. His hand is supple and quick as he arcs his pencil over the page.

Just to be here with a sketchbook on his lap and a beer at his feet is ample reason for heartfelt gratitude. There are so many forces operating on a man, influencing his behaviour and determining his attitudes, that it's hard to adopt a stance in life. What relieves Max even more than knowing that he has at last found a niche, is the fact that the women in his life, behind him at this very moment, each in various stages of orgasmic rapture, like him just as he is— unreservedly, for his abilities and his understanding.

Only days ago, he had started the Harley with a habitual twist of the throttle and felt the burn of self-consciousness at the fatuous roaring from the exhaust. He would sell it, if Phoebe didn't like it so much. The clinch of her arms around him as they soar over the ranges thrills him almost as much as having sex with her for love.

Max has been pursuing a train of thought for some time now, and today, with his attention devoted to eliciting designs on human skin, in an emporium suffused with carnal tension, it came to him—what they are doing is art. Not the tattoos and the henna, but rather, the Thrum experience.

True art transforms—it elucidates new ideas and attitudes. If art is the expression of the emerging consciousness in the human environment, through which we create, from seeming chaos, a poetic sensibility of our changing times, then what is happening at the Glamorama is art. Because, Max is in no doubt that an incipient mindfulness is replacing the conventions by which the townsfolk have always led their lives.

Behind the settee, seated in one of the Thrum chairs, Angela takes a long guzzle of her beer, then puts it on the bench and nestles into the seat.

Beside her is Denise, with a beer in her lap, her eyes closed and the fronds of her incredibly long eyelashes motionless against her cheek. She makes a small adjustment of the controller, which makes her lashes flutter.

Next in the line of chairs is Tiffany, drinking a gin and tonic through a straw, so as not to dislodge the face pack she has plastered to her.

Then, there is Phoebe, with the controls on her chair set to launch position.

Phoebe's chin slowly rises and her lips part. The bottle of beer she holds in her lap starts to froth and cascade all over her hand.

A Delicate State of Affairs

So, in the end, it all came together—in a manner of speaking. It was a secret... and it wasn't a secret. People found out about it and were either curious to know more, or were repulsed. But, whatever their feelings, the subject was so fraught with controversy and possible bad fall-out, that town gossip for a long while contained all manner of allusions and intimations, as the residents weighed up one another.

Sally, from the Mustering Yard—the hardest working and most sincere person one could ever hope to meet—was the only vocal critic. Which was a bit awkward, seeing as how she was just across the road from the Glamorama. Her disapproval derived from a staunch belief in common decency; she adhered faithfully to her principles because that was the way she had been brought up. And no one held that against her; it was just that, whenever she did in some way allude to the goings on inside the salon, people were so daunted by the scope of the subject that they were, effectively, rendered mute.

The Thrum experience was outrageous; it was also highly desirable, and way too many people were implicated for ill-considered questions to be asked.

And this delicate state applied just to the population of women; for a while, the blokes didn't know where they stood. There was a period of time when manly gravitas teetered on the brink of alcoholism.

Philosophy

Inside the pub, the bar is softly lit. Men lean with elbows on the counter and jostle around the tables in boisterous conversation. There is a prevailing eagerness in the faces, a boyish innocence that so often becomes clouded by the travails of adolescence and the demands of manhood. In one corner is a group gathered around a guitar player singing Sam Cooke's *Wonderful World*. '*... don't know much about history...*'

Janice's husband Mal is leaning with his back against the bar, holding open a copy of their cookbook—*TOP CHOPS*. A number of men are leaning over and craning their necks for a view. Some of them interact with fellow gourmands, animatedly slicing, stirring, sprinkling and dicing the air.

The barman flicks the top off a bottle of home-made beer. The label reads—STREWTH.

Len, a roo shooter who makes smoked and cured game, passes around a platter.

The guitarist in the corner is joined by an accordion player and a fiddler. Soon, irresistible Celtic rhythms erupt as the musicians' fingers fly over their instruments. The bar is littered with empty bottles of

Strewth. The crowd is becoming even more garrulous.

A group of soccer players in their new STRIKERS jerseys earnestly expound upon the existential qualities of struggle as opposed to winning and losing. Unable to take credit for the mixed-team's new-found form, the men have begun to colour their conversation with a self-deprecating humour, and in place of a sense of dire fatalism, they have developed a brusque irreverence for sport as a metaphor.

Max and Ian lean against the bar with a large format book on archaeology open between them. They examine one of the colour plates of a stone idol, round and fat, with enormous breasts and a clearly defined and prominent vulva. Max's tattooed hand smooths over the page.

Ian harks back his head and says with a preposterous snort, 'Orgasm?'

Max's reply is succinct, 'Orgasm.'

Ian grimaces with doubt, 'That says orgasm to you? I thought it was a fertility symbol... a fertility figurine.'

Max rolls his eyes, 'Well yeah! That's how the stuffy old Victorian archaeologists interpreted it. You can't imagine them rolling up to Queen Vickie with this in their hand, and saying, "Your Majesty, we believe the ancients venerated the female orgasm" now, can you?'

Their heads close together as they study the photo thoroughly.

Ian scratches his nose. 'Well, no... possibly not. But, I still don't see how that says orgasm.'

Max gives an empty gesture with his hands.

'Perhaps it doesn't, Ian. But think about this—this figure is utterly common. It doesn't embody any features of particular beauty—no adornments, no clothing, no symbols. Not even a face—it was never made with a face.' Max articulates his next words very clearly, 'It's very, very ordinary—apart from the obvious fact that she is fat, has large breasts and a prominent vulva.'

The barman and a few patrons nearby abandon their discussions to listen in.

Ian looks unimpressed. 'She's pregnant!'

Max waves his finger in Ian's face. 'Not necessarily. That is not necessarily a pregnant bulge. Think of all the societies that admire big women—and pregnancy would have been better shown with a bulge low down—a more obviously pregnant bulge.'

'But the large bosom then—surely a symbol of an ability to nurture—to provide.'

With a hint of impatience, Max takes a deep breath. 'Not really, Ian. As you must know, breast size has little to do with milk supply and this would have been well-established knowledge in the supposedly difficult times in which our forebears lived...'

'But a symbol then,' interrupts Ian, 'I mean, if you're going to use breasts as a symbol of nurturing, then...' he uses his hands to illustrate his point, 'well, you'd make prominent breasts.'

Quite a few more heads in the crowd turn to listen.

Max slaps shut the book. 'Look, forget about the breasts for a moment...'

One of the listeners gives a small pout of

disappointment.

'... consider this—if the objective of this statue was to invoke the beneficence of the Gods...'

Ian delicately interjects, 'Christ, Max! Where'd you learn those words?'

Max raises an ominous brow. 'Hey, the tattoos are superficial... but I like to think that I go...'

Ian reaches out to Max's shoulder and cuts him short. 'Sorry, Max. I'm sorry. I didn't mean to... go on!'

Max smiles and makes himself comfortable against the bar. Most of the men are listening now. For all their coarseness of feature, they are naturally intrigued by the mystery of the female.

'Why, going on our past history of making graven images in the likenesses of our gods, is this image so ordinary? So unsophisticated? Why is it not *like* a god? Why didn't the ancients make their appeals to a representation of their god—some supernatural, winged-thing—terrifying, muscular, all-powerful entity shooting bolts of lightning? Why would they venerate their fat wives?'

Many in the crowd sagely nod their heads.

Ian cautiously looks about. 'Well, why then, Max?'

Max is now aware that everyone's attention is on him, and for a moment, the familiar feeling of dread clutches at his chest. But now, it's different. He knows what he wants to say; it's there lying open in his heart; a truth that is so easy to behold and so easy to give, that it takes no courage at all—only love.

Ever so slightly, the men around him surge with

anticipation.

'Because...' he eyes the faces mischievously, 'women *are* gods; they have a supernatural feature—the orgasm. It's completely useless and overwhelmingly enjoyable—and, it's what it is that can make humanity truly civilized.'

Amidst the weighty consideration that this engenders, someone says uncertainly, '... the clitoris?'

Max leans back on the bar and, with his elbows on the edge, steeples his fingers across his stomach. 'Imagine,' he says with deliberation, 'a community that understood completely, human sexuality—a community that among its members, had, for want of a better word, priests and priestesses whose purpose it was to guide young couples through the celebration of marriage—to instruct and inform them of the accumulated cultural wisdom to do with living together—successfully and productively...'

The listeners stroke stubbly chins, wipe beer froth from their mouths, blink with concentration and furrow weathered brows.

'... and, upon completion of the celebration of marriage, the wedding, they were each given a figurine, for them to place above the hearth,' Max holds up the book with the picture of the stone figurine, 'to remind them of their divinity to each other—to remind them to celebrate their sexual union—sex! Because, good sex... really good sex, of the mind and body, is good not just for them, but for the whole community.'

There is an elfin bravura in the way Max challenges

his audience, and grandeur in the way he reveals a sublime truth. At last, the sensibilities of the art student are free to be expressed; the words that he has avoided for so long because he thought they stigmatised him, are there on his tongue, waiting.

'... and it's not about fertility. I think we can assume that most couples would have been sufficiently fertile to obviate the need to worship fat dolls. Anyway, there are better ways to suggest fertility; a mother and her baby—a family group. No, these statuettes, both male and female, are overtly sexual in the most decent and sincere way. If, in those times, few people could read, how could they say, "sex is special"? How could they say, "love each other"? How else could they say, "orgasm"?'

Magic

The institution of morning tea must be responsible for significant developments in our culture. We are at our freshest then, fully awake, with the trials of the day yet to burden us; it is the most optimistic of occasions.

Out on the footpath in front of the bakery, al fresco and joyous, a party of women—mothers, daughters, neighbours and friends—are forging a new expression of female bonding that derives its inspiration from the power of individuality. Keeping in mind that this is a time-worn country town, the sight of bohemian attire— lavish headwear, brightly coloured suits, cravats and various other adornments—is considered very novel. What supports this display of colour is the discovery that, through embracing individuality, diversity will flourish, and with it, the answers to all our conflicts.

There is nothing subdued about the host of ladies enjoying the sidewalk café; they are seated at maison wrought iron settings, sipping from Limoges Elite Demitasse teacups, and the pale winter sunshine alights on their happy faces. They laugh as Moira recounts outrageous stories about her experiences on the stage, and regales them with scandalous yarns about her days as a gorgeous young and privileged student at the most prestigious private school in Melbourne.

'... and so, I simply squared my shoulders and looked as defiant as a sixteen-year-old can look, and blurted out, "Miss Ireland, I am *not* playing Don Quixote! Choose Margarette—she has a naturally androgynous appearance and is far better suited to playing a man— or his beast"...'

There is much delighted clapping and small displays of intimacy between the listeners as they hang from Moira's every word.

'... of course, the *pursuit* of culture is a sanctimonious affectation that leaves us isolated and bereft of relevance in life. Culture is the score marks left from an abrasive and imperative contact with the world; all the best examples of working culture exhibit this gritty reality.'

Some of the ladies are wearing items of clothing that could only have come from the Empire Fashion House. Confirmation of this is visible in the display window where a beautifully hand written placard, proclaims—*Affordable Prices*.

Across the street, Ellen and Ian look through the window of the hardware at the happy occasion.

'So, tell me, Ellen, why haven't we seen you in the salon? Why haven't they, I mean. I don't... hardly... just to fix...'

Ellen's wistful smile broadens as she ponders a

165

reply. 'Oh, I don't think that I'll get around to it.'

Ian is unaware of his naivety on most occasions, and this harmless exchange is a case in point.

'You should. I think you'd enjoy it.'

The two of them look out of the window for a while longer.

Ellen faces her long-time friend. 'I wouldn't enjoy having my hair cut, Ian.'

Ian clearly doesn't understand. 'Well, a manicure then. I don't expect you'd want a tattoo... um, anywhere...' He inadvertently glances at Ellen's cleavage.

Ellen gives a little laugh and pulls downwards at the material of her blouse. She looks at the whiteness of the top of her breast and gives a pout of consideration. 'Hmmm... perhaps. Maybe a brace and bit, or...' she pulls the material down some more, 'two bags of grout.'

Behind the shame on Ian's face, there's a fair amount of rejoicing too. He raises his sight to a particularly bright corner of the window in order to have an excuse to squint. He remains looking at the glare.

Ellen leans nearer to him. 'Do you remember the accident, Ian?'

Ian narrows his gaze to the brightest reflection on the window. 'Of course, I do.' The light is pure and empty. 'You almost died at the bottom of that bridge. No one's fault—wasn't Ron's fault. It was an accident— the place was notorious for roos—and you were the

166

most beautiful girl in the school.'

Ellen touches Ian's wrist with her fingertips. 'Well, there are the scars that you can see, and...' she searches Ian's face, 'the scars that would prevent me from enjoying having my hair cut.' She laughs at her little joke.

Ian tries hard to conceal his anguish. 'I didn't know that, Ellen.'

'No one does.' Ellen's eyes dart to the back of the shop where occasional noises hint at the presence of Ron. Ian looks down at Ellen's hands, spread palms down on the counter. Unable to make eye contact, he covers her hands with his and surveys the space behind the counter that used to be clear and tidy. Now, it is a clutter of messy paint tins, brushes in buckets, rolls of masking tape, a paint-spattered drop sheet and a hand steady.

With her characteristic lopsidedness, Ellen smiles at Ian's touch. The scars pull not just at her eye, but at the perception of herself.

After the plunge from the bridge, Ellen regained consciousness to find that she had not lost her life, not a limb, nor even her new platform shoes—but she had lost her good looks. She wasn't vain; she wasn't even really aware that she had been good-looking; but now she knew she wasn't. She didn't dwell morbidly on that fact. She knew she was lucky to be alive—many people, before and since, had died at that terrible place. It's just that she didn't feel anything anymore; she had lost the sensual connection between herself and the world.

She no longer painted; creating images, especially of beauty, seemed pointless. All of this existed behind the scars in her mind.

Then Ian had come along. Not the preoccupied inventor who embarrassed himself with inappropriate glances, but the soulful genius who had accidentally created alchemy and who had the humility to make it real for everyone—including Ellen.

'You have created magic, Ian—after all these years.'

Ian's throat is tight with ineffable sadness. 'Ah, well, it's not actually me that's performing the magic, Ellen.'

The two of them stay motionless. The sunlight streams into the shop on delicate beams of dust.

'Don't be sad for me. Your magic has touched me too.' She moves to one side and sweeps her arm to reveal what's behind her. 'Look—I've started painting again.'

More clutter comes into view for Ian. A stepladder, paint trays and a sketchbook, open to reveal animals in playful disorder and another sketch, of the bakery, with designs for a mural concept of a wild and rampant passionfruit vine.

Ian is drawn to the vine and its glossy leaves; it's so much like the one that has taken over at his place. The sun is producing more glare than ever now, but it's not just the sun that is blurring his vision. He closes his eyes and allows himself to float timelessly with the warmth on his face. A voice exhorts him to look. He doesn't want to. The voice is insistent, so he summons the energy to lift his eyelids.

A perfect face with porcelain white skin is looking at him. Strangely expressionless, it goads him to pay attention, moving in and out and tilting provocatively in his vision. He tries to say something, but his voice is sabotaged with emotion. Then he recognizes the voice—it is Ellen.

'... it's not too perfect is it, Ian? My father brought it back from Japan after the war. I thought I might wear it to the ball next week... hmmm? What do you think?'

Ian whispers roughly, 'No. No, it's not too perfect, Ellen. Not for you.'

Ellen's good side sparkles. 'Oh, good!'

She puts the Geisha mask back under the bench. Then, she cants her face before Ian's bowed head and runs a hand through his hair, feeling the thinning strands. 'You know, Ian—you're right. I can't go to the ball without paying a visit to the Glamorama.'

Ian wipes away the tears from his face.

Modelling

Inside the Glamorama it is deathly quiet. Ellen opens one of the light boxes and gives an involuntary jump as the spring-loaded latches snap against the lid. She looks around the vast emporium, beyond the Thrum chairs and through the window, out into the street. It is too early on a Sunday for anyone to be about, and seeing that it's raining, it's not likely that the street will get busy. Her gaze rests on the pastel-coloured chairs and she wonders about the strategy of keeping the salon so visible to passers-by. From the footpath, the view inside is not *completely* unobstructed; there are numerous art works, pot plants and displays to impede scrutiny, but nonetheless, Ellen recoils inwardly at the thought of customers in an orgasmic thrall being so exposed to unwitting pedestrians.

Phoebe had said something about encouraging clients to maintain a sense of decorum, and that the proximity of the outside world reminded them not to become too abandoned.

The very back of the emporium has a space that suits Ellen's needs, and she sets about assembling the light stands around a large square of carpet that

Phoebe had rolled out for her the day before. She switches on the lamps and checks the readings on the light meter.

All good.

She snaps shut the cover but remains staring at the bright halo on the carpet. She recalls Ian's tormented face as she peered at him through the geisha mask. She had made him cry.

Poor Ian... he hasn't yet realised how much my life has changed.

People had come to her for requests: to paint a new sign, to decorate a window, to brighten a mailbox, do a mural. She sensed the change in the community just at that time when she desperately wanted to change herself. That was Ian's magic; he had made it easier for her. And now, she was dabbing and brushing again— not high art, but fun, lively images in acrylics. She felt herself being restored. Ron had told her that he didn't want her to be in the shop; he wanted to be able to look out of the window and see her painting the town.

And then, late one afternoon, Phoebe had walked into the hardware and told her that she wanted to have the huge façade of the Glamorama painted and did she have any suggestions. Ellen had become aware of the story of the origin of the Thrum chairs—the principal players. The idea came to her almost immediately—a mural of the three women—*in a sort of swirling entwinement... psychedelic... to represent the... you know...*

Phoebe loved it and commissioned it on the spot.

171

Ellen said she would require a photo session.

'Not a problem—in the Glamorama on Sunday—here's the key.'

Now she had two reasons to visit the salon: a promise to Ian and a photo shoot.

To Ellen, the Glamorama still felt out of bounds. Where initially she'd borne a vague resentment at the ability of others to reinvent themselves, now she didn't want there to be any misperception. She had only just rediscovered her passion and her means of expression because of her reconciliation of the past. Visiting the Glamorama, and the implication that she had been initiated to the joys of the Thrum chair, would compromise what she had been able to achieve.

Voices intrude into her thoughts.

Phoebe, Tiffany and Sonya stroll to the back of the emporium and greet Ellen with effusive hugs.

For an awkward moment, Ellen is at a loss as to where to begin, and to gain time, she reflectively appraises the carpet with a finger on her lips. 'Um, I was thinking, maybe if...' but when she turns around, the three women have completely disrobed and are waiting expectantly for directions in their underwear.

'Just in case you want more of our bodies in the mural,' Sonya says. She steps forward and kneels down onto the carpet then lies down towards one side of the square.

Tiffany comes and sprawls down beside her, spreading her long hair through her fingers. Phoebe lies down on the other side of Tiffany so that the three faces are framed by the lustrous whorls of Tiffany's tresses. The three of them look up at Ellen, blinking as they accustom to the lights. The glow of the lamps is reflected in their lipsticks.

The composition of the palette is golden. Ellen's doubts evaporate. She grabs her camera and steps in amongst the bodies. She peers through the lens. Tiffany's face is a blur, before it comes into sharp focus. She is looking straight at the camera with a look of constrained mirth.

Ellen's speech is muffled by the camera body. 'Make her laugh, Phoebe.'

Phoebe clears her throat. 'Well, I was thinking—can you have too many orgasms?'

Tiffany giggles, 'Oh, Phoebe!'

'Thanks, Phoebe. Nice, Tiff. Nice.' The auto-wind whirs.

Out of view, Sonya says, 'I hope so, Phoebe. I hate to think that I might die without reaching my potential.'

Tiffany stays composed. 'Phoebes—are you developing a callus?'

'Very funny, Tiff. No, I was just wondering whether, well... do we have a duty of care? You know... to our clients.'

Ellen zooms in on Tiffany. 'Okay, Tiff—what have you got!'

In an instant, Tiffany's face is wreathed in a look of ecstasy. She curls her lip in a languorous snarl and bares a little of her lovely teeth.

The camera clicks and whines. 'Great, Tiff. Look at

the lens.'

Tiffany looks longingly at the camera and chews at her lip.

'Good... good,' breathes Ellen. 'Very, um... natural.'

Phoebe murmurs sarcastically in Tiffany's ear, 'Enjoy your work then, do you?'

Tiffany bursts out laughing and clutches her hands to her face.

The camera rattles off shots with mechanical fluidity.

Ellen shifts the lens to Sonya.

With a distant look, Sonya says, 'Do you think we all experience the same thing?'

'I doubt it,' Phoebe scoffs, 'we're all different.'

'But, not *that* different—surely,' Tiffany poses.

Ellen bends down and, from a compact, brushes a little rouge onto Sonya's cheeks.

Phoebe sighs deeply, as if about to reveal something in strictest confidence. 'Look, all I know is that the other afternoon, when Miranda had... passed out in her chair, well, I turned off the controller, but left the settings as they were, and, before I locked up, I tried it out.'

'And?' the other two chorus.

'Well, when I switched it on, it felt like I'd disturbed a flock of pigeons.'

Tiffany squeals with laughter. Sonya, still in the field of the lens, seems transported by the thought of new dimensions to her orgasms. She turns to the camera, her face alight with anticipated rapture.

Ellen's voice is barely above a whisper, 'Oh, yes, Sonya, that's great... lovely... now, go all the way... all the way.'

The camera clicks repeatedly as Sonya sighs, her sweet face dissolving into bliss.

Ellen stays locked to the camera. 'Blow me a kiss, sweetheart.'

Sonya cups both hands to her chin and blows a fat kiss to the lens.

'Perfect.'

Ellen pans across to Phoebe whose dark eyes sparkle with mischief.

Tiffany blurts out, 'But did you like it?'

Phoebe eyes the camera with smug consideration. 'Hmmm, I think I could get a taste for it.' A smirk lingers on her lips.

Tiffany says, with sudden seriousness, 'Do you think it's addictive? I mean, what you said about duty of care. Do you think the ladies won't be able to control their habit?'

Ellen reaches down and flicks at a stray lock of Phoebe's hair. 'You'll all end up at Orgasms Anonymous.'

The three women shriek with laughter. With adroit steps, Ellen manoeuvres around them, squeezing off shots in all directions. The continuous rattle and whine of the camera is inaudible, the women are laughing so hard.

'—hello, my name is Tiffany and I'm an orgasmaholic!'

'—and I don't stop... don't stop... don't stop...'

Sonya moans.

They writhe and paw at each other.

Ellen checks her camera. The finished roll is being automatically rewound.

The models compose themselves with huge sighs and raucous coughing. They sit up and adjust their underwear.

Ellen surveys the trio, looking a little awkward and vulnerable. 'Well, I think that was successful. I've got more than enough to go on.'

Phoebe levers herself off the floor and moves towards one of the lamps. Casually she points it towards Ellen.

With a finely tuned reflex, Ellen turns her head so that one side of her face remains in shadow.

Phoebe moves towards her and places her hand on Ellen's shoulder. The two other women get up and gather near her.

Tiffany gently takes one of Ellen's hands. 'It's your turn now.'

'Yeah? Well, I don't know if I can be as comfortably public about this as you obviously are.'

'It's no big deal, Ellen,' Phoebe says, 'it's no different from being in a restaurant where people are enjoying fine food. We don't pass by with a smug, secret little smile and think "I know what you're enjoying." No, if people are enjoying their food, good luck to them.'

'Bon appetit!' Sonya adds.

With a wan smile, Ellen lifts the hand she is holding with Tiffany over her heart. Phoebe and Sonya cover her hand with theirs.

Ellen's gaze travels to the Thrum chairs at the front of the salon. Beyond them, through the display windows, the rain has become heavier. There won't be a soul out on the street.

Phoebe twirls a lock of Ellen's hair in her free hand and fingers it with professional scrutiny.

Girls

Sonya told me that they spent that rainy afternoon reclining in the chairs, provocatively regaling each other, with none of the chairs switched on except Ellen's. They'd pushed the chairs, which are on large felt pads, into a circle, mixed themselves some sort of frothy cocktail, then told Ellen that they weren't going to stop drinking until she'd had a bit of a go—even if it meant all of them getting blind drunk. Ellen surprised them by saying she could easily drink all of them under the table, but that she was happy to have a go just to see what all the fuss was about.

Of course, it was all bluster, the girls talking like that; here were four women, working out how to make contact in, as Ellen herself declared, the realm of empathetic eroticism—when arousal and altruism meld. And, apparently, it's not just sexual arousal alone, but elevation of any human endeavour that has an erotic component to it, be it sport or architecture, music or gastronomy; erotica is in everything we do in life that is beautiful.

Of course, she was a little way along in the Thrum chair by then, and the others were too tiddly to reason

178

with her, so who knows what wisdom came and went in the low glow of the Glamorama.

White Wedding

The leaves of the passionfruit vine are luxuriantly green and lush with arcing tendrils searching for places to grasp. The flower is fat and white with an almost iridescent purple centre—in fact, it is slightly iridescent because it is not a real flower but a painted mural on the façade of Iris's newly named, Passion Parlour.

Laughter and conversation emanate from the sidewalk café, now incorporating the pavement in front of the, also newly named, Empress Fashion Boutique.

It is a warm spring noon. Iris emerges from her establishment dressed as her dream hybrid of parlourmaid and sex kitten. She struts between the crowded tables holding aloft an exquisite silver tray crammed with assorted baked sweets.

The passionfruit vine extends to the Empress Fashion Boutique, curling a few tentative tendrils over the royal blue façade.

Iris puts down the tray at a large table, to appreciative sounds by the gathering.

The last of the winter wind gusts fleetingly around the party, flapping tablecloths and making people hug themselves with the frisson of anticipation.

Sonya gives Ian's hand a pat. 'Ian? We're ready.' She has an aura of confidence, in the jut of her chin and the curl of her smile. Her eyes crinkle with the humour that she has had her whole life.

The two of them look expectantly at the portal of the boutique.

Ellen, seated demurely next to Ron, leans against his shoulder, her softly permed locks falling loosely over one side of her face. He whispers in her ear and she laughs out loud.

Max is not wearing leather, nor black. He attempts to gag Phoebe who is trying to steal the punch line from an incident that he is recounting to someone standing behind them.

Tiffany rummages under her seat for her handbag. She reaches behind her and gives Jane and her friend a few coins. Her skirt rides up with the motion and reveals her lovely, tanned thighs. The girls scamper off. Beside her, sunburnt and lanky, Len looks on at the exchange, and when the girls have gone, he places his arm around Tiffany's shoulder and hugs her near.

Janice and Mal are there, happy and exalted.

Miranda is wearing a man's smoking jacket in grey silk, sufficiently low-cut to amply display her large breasts, one with a tattoo of the moon and the other with a tattoo of the sun and, about them, a galaxy of tiny, perfect stars. Beside her, with her hand resting on Miranda's knee, is Siobhan, wearing a sequined slip from the flapper era, complete with a tiara featuring a tiny, stylised swift in flight.

Claire is looking stunning in a floral, fifties frock, holding tightly to her man, he with his arm casually resting on her shoulder, a red rose in his grip.

Angela and her beau are each holding a wildly coiffured lapdog in their arms.

Others are there: Hannah and her husband, he toying with the wedding ring on her finger; Lynne, with a beautiful swan torc around her upper arm; Bettina, flushed with a satiated radiance being embraced by Nick; Maggie, looking ever so sweet as she clutches hold of her husband; Phil with his wife dreamily draped in his lap as they share a seat.

A moment of calm transpires and all eyes gravitate to the boutique. The display in the window is fabulous; eccentrically dressed mannequins combine bold body art and sharp, lurid hairstyles with high fashion from the 1930s.

Moira's assistant steps down from the entrance onto the pavement and waits.

All eyes are on the arched doorway. From within the shadows, Moira emerges to stand in the entrance wearing, what must surely be, the wedding dress of the Queen Mother from 1923.

The onlookers are beside themselves with hilarity. Max dashes out and escorts Moira down the steps to the pavement. Moira's assistant deftly holds the train aloft as Moira parades around the group, clutching in her hands a posy of colourful flowers. Women hug themselves, and others, as the cheering and laughter rings out.

The pageant ends in front of Ian's seat. With an imperious mien on her perfectly-made face, Moira stands before Ian and bestows him a long look. Then, with a dolorous drawl, she says, 'Cheers, Ian...' and delicately throws the spray of flowers into his lap.

More laughter erupts as Ian and Sonya, their foreheads touching, sniff the flowers.

Hands

Yep, we sat there in front of Iris's Passion Parlour and laughed and laughed about how little it took to make a change. It felt really good to laugh with the people that had come into my life—that had always been in my life. And I know that it is possible to love more than just one person; of course it is—it would be illogical for it not to be so. We choose to make the commitment to one, special person because it allows us to develop a relationship into a workable partnership that will endure and be creative throughout our lives. Though, if the truth be told, one's life-partner reflects oneself, and we all like to see our reflection. Every tiny advancement, every self-indulgent triumph, every humble conquest that one makes from day to day is reflected to us by our partner; it engenders the most authentic form of self-actualization.

And, while I'm perfectly aware that the distance between the other loves in my life may heighten the illusion of love, it also spares me the tedium of cloying domesticity.

I make a point of watching the hands responsible for the changes in our town; it's what we do that is the most emphatic statement of ourselves; it's a physical world that requires a physical touch. Hands seem, to me at least, such evocative indicators of personality. If the opposing thumb is the reason for our intellect, then the shape of the hand reveals our soul.

There is no more privileged work than that which involves touching another person, and it should always be considered a magical moment; the hands that assist, that beautify, that soothe and calm are the ways in which we confirm our civilization.

And me? I'm just an instrument of something greater, and happy to be, too—more than happy to be.

I am left with many strong images from the time that we embarked on this, as I said earlier, scarcely believable journey. For instance, I can clearly see the Thrum control panel embedded into the soft leather of a chair. A woman's fingers trace across the glinting metal as she returns her hand to her lap. She toys with the fabric of her skirt, causing it to travel up from her knee. Her legs are immaculately hairless and her shins a little shiny from such dedicated depilation. Freckles, scars and blemishes dapple her skin like a tapestry all the way to her pale, bare feet, where Tiffany expertly applies lacquer to the woman's perfectly trimmed toenails.

I'm happy for Tiffany. I love that girl—after what we shared. And, she loves people. Yes, she does.

Then, there were times when I entered the Glamorama for some urgent repair job. I have an image of soft, downy curls at the nape of a woman's neck, still her original colour, and Phoebe, taking care not to apply unnecessary dye there. Her client has her head bent forward at quite an acute angle, a position that Phoebe discovered works well to abate the exertions of the climax and which helps to maintain a degree of seemliness in the salon. She wipes the small amount of dye up into the hair, then, with a dexterous movement, she sheds her gloves and gently massages the woman's heaving shoulders.

I love Phoebe, too. She has an indomitable spirit, that girl, and God knows we need people like her if we're to survive.

And, I see Max's sinewy hand, holding his client's breast up and out of the way from where he is applying the tattoo pen. 'I love you, Max... I love you...' she implores him with a quiver in her voice.

I was underneath one of the massage tables at the time, replacing a circuit board that had overheated. I could see and overhear everything; Max bending his head closer to her chest and murmuring, 'I love you too, baby. Now just be still... be still...' as his pen filled in the colour of a tiny, open book just over his client's heart. 'I love you, Max,' she whispered over and over.

I have so much admiration for Max— the way he has changed. It's important for all of us.

I love Moira. Wow—has she changed! I had no idea that ninety-year-olds could feel such... so much... Well, anyway, she's unique. Completely cured of her palsy by the way—visits the salon most weeks, even though she can do her own make-up again.

And Ellen; it wrenches my heart each time I see her. I remember when she was painting the huge mural above the awning of the Glamorama. Ron and I looked up and followed a glistening trail of paint as she dragged her brush in a gleaming arc through a loose tangle of similar curves. It was a skein of hair. Up there, the setting sun saturated the vast extent of the façade in a reddish glow. She clung to the scaffold, swept back her own hair and called down to Ron for his opinion. I so vividly recall the look of adoration on his face as he gave her a two-thumbs-up. Ellen mouthed us each a kiss. The entire gable end was bedecked with the faces of women in ecstasy: mouths sensuously open, hands to cheeks, biting knuckles, running fingers through hair, licking lips, chewing lips, lifting breasts, arching throats, looking with languor and longing and... Sonya, blushed and golden, blowing a kiss.

Most of all, I love Sonya with all my heart. I can still see her tucked up in bed with a sheet right to her chin, after that, you know, incident in the shed. She was reborn—all pink and rosy and helpless. I love her because... she's a woman. Well, of course she's a woman, but what I mean is that, there's something powerful about being a woman, and it's not about using your sexuality as a weapon. It's about being part of a greater humanity.

I mean, think about it—women don't need to go into ecstasy to conceive, right! The survival of the species is assured even if women were bored rigid with the thought of sex. Men would always connive and beg to get their way... when they weren't raping and pillaging.

I don't know why things are the way they are. All I know is that we have not yet fully explored what we are capable of. But here, in our proper, country town, I have been in wonder at what I have witnessed, and though nothing has changed on the outside—apart from Ellen's murals—everything has changed on the inside.

I think—and remember, I'm an inventor—I think we are at a nodal point in the feminine energy field. We all experience it, but women can access this energy in a unique way. And when they do, phew! Anything's possible. And when they are denied—we get religion. Hah! No, just kidding. I can feel it in me—all men have it in varying degrees. Max had it all along.

Ah, I don't know—maybe I'm just getting very mellow with age—none of that old testosterone coursing through my balls, or wherever it courses— though Tiffany would have something to say about that, I imagine. That's the trouble with men's sexuality— it has an evolutionary imperative; they can't help themselves. Mind you, if we invented a men's titillator, we'd be on it for two minutes and spend the rest of the day at the pub, and where would the human race be then?

I've come to the conclusion that the female climax is definitely creative and, paradoxically, not necessary for maintaining the species. So, it's a gift. Like Max said, a gift to all humanity.

Masks

It is the night of the masked ball. The band is in full swing. The hall is ablaze with colour. Thousands of streamers loop down from the ceiling and the walls are decorated with bright designs—from butterflies to bon-bons—stars to stallions. Under the hot, yellow glow of the lamps, the movement of the crowd is mesmerizing as the dancers reel around the floor.

The passionfruit flower is glossy and bright and part of a mask in which the petals slant down and cover Tiffany's face. She raises her hand to her mouth and blows a kiss. Then, tipping the mask to one side with her fingers, she exposes her whole face. She blinks both eyes in a knowing and mischievous wrinkle before being whisked away by her partner. They meld into the throng of gyrating dancers, lost in the pulse and flow of the music.

It's jazz, big and sumptuous and the female vocalist, shining with perspiration, digs deep as she renders the bridge in *Until the Real Thing Comes Along*.

Ian is wearing a mask made to appear as though it is constructed from riveted iron plates. He looks a little like the Tin Man as he holds Sonya close. The impassive mechanical detachment is just an illusion, because behind the metal lids, Ian's eyes are closed and tearing. Sonya lazily spins him around. Her mask has a Tibetan princess theme featuring a third eye in the forehead. She reaches up and plants a lingering kiss on Ian's grey mask, leaving a fat, red lip-print.

Through the crowd, Horus, the Egyptian god of kings, lifts his glass from behind his woman's back and offers Ian a silent toast. Max tweaks the falcon mask just enough for him to wink at Phoebe, who has on a cheeky little devil mask, bright red with two little horns protruding either side of the devil's wrinkled forehead. The fact is, there is a certain ambiguity about the appearance of the mask and a lot of people, upon spying the tiny third horn hidden amongst the folds on the forehead, blush self-consciously.

A disturbingly flawless face gazes over a man's shoulder as he diffidently steps to the rhythm of the music. She beckons with the hand around his neck for the viewer to come closer. She's a Geisha, but with brown, wavy hair piled to one side. She clasps her hand across her face and pulls the expressionless porcelain visage away. Ellen entwines a lock of her hair around a finger then puts the finger to her lips, conspiring to hold the viewer to secrecy. Then, she laughs as she spins away.

Miranda's mask is the sun and the moon side by side with bright little stars all around.

Iris is wearing a tiny mask with heavily made-up eyes, where one of the long-lashed eyelids winks repeatedly with spring-loaded smoothness.

Angela's crazily coiffured hair almost hides her truck wheels mask.

Claire has a guitar shaped yellow mask—sun yellow—Thrum yellow, if you like.

Janice's mask has peacock feathers spraying out the side.

The face behind the baby face mask is that of Moira and the juxtaposition when she reveals herself is quite shocking.

The band pauses in its rhythm for the singer to linger over the last few bars.

...and if that isn't love, I'll just have to wait, until the real thing comes along...

One Sunny Morning

Well, there you go. All I can say is that I'm so very, very happy for the Goddesses in my life—for everyone in the little town of Thrum.

Yep, a rumour started circulating that the town was going to be renamed. As usual, I was the last person to know. And then, one day, I was driving back into town, and there it was—a sturdy signpost—had to have been made by Public Works—six by six hardwood post— lettering routed into two-inch thick board—black writing on white, as per government specs. I drove through the main street, beside the railway, to the other side of town. Same thing there—a sturdy signpost declaring that I now lived in the township of Thrum.

A lot of questions roiled in my mind, but I didn't want to let on that I was uninformed, so I prepared a conspiratorial smirk ready to use in the course of conversation. But, I never had to, because no one ever mentioned a thing about it—until the day of the naming ceremony.

It was a Sunday morning and I was sitting on the stool in my shed. The roller door was open and I was daydreaming, looking out onto the street. Across the road, Neville and Gwen strolled out onto their front lawn and stopped to take in the morning sun. They then commenced walking hand in hand along the footpath. They waved to me and I waved back. Something glinted in their hands, but I couldn't make out what it was. Soon after, another couple, and then another, walked past, giving me a cheery, glinting wave as they went by. Then, Tiffany walked past the roller door. She smiled, but didn't stop. She twirled something bright in her hand at me—it was a champagne flute. I walked out of the shed onto the footpath and looked towards Tiffany's departing form. I saw that there were lots of people out walking, all converging at the street corner and continuing on towards the centre of town.

I saw Sonya, out on the road verge in front of our house. She was looking straight at me and beckoned me with her head. I walked over and noticed that she had two champagne flutes in her hand. 'This one's for you,' she said as I reached her.

I was completely at a loss. 'What's going on?' I asked.

Sonya smiled and held out her hand for me to take. 'You'll see,' she said.

Well, we walked, in an ever-growing congregation, towards town. It was one of those gorgeous autumn mornings where the day is so still, it seems to settle around you. Everywhere I looked, people's champagne glasses sparkled in their hands. Up ahead, I noticed that the columns of people were not heading into the main street, but instead, were turning to follow the road out of town. For a brief moment, I had this thought that I was being railroaded, and that the citizens were going to celebrate as soon as I crossed the bridge. But, I definitely didn't see any hostility in the faces around me—though it was eerie that everyone seemed to be so self-absorbed. There wasn't a voice to be heard; we all crunched resolutely along on the side of the road.

The marching became hypnotic for me. The road turned and the sun shone in our faces. I honestly had no idea what was going on; I began to feel a welling of emotion; we were all heading in the same direction. I was overcome with a powerful sense of unity. I bowed my head and began to plod. Sonya shouldered me onward. 'Almost there,' she said.

Gradually, the sounds diminished, and when I looked up, there were hundreds of people standing around the approach to the bridge. They were looking at the new sign.

Sonya led me to the front of the gathering. Moira was standing on a platform right next to the sign. It seemed much bigger, now that I was seeing it close up. Someone grabbed my arm and lifted it. My glass was filled. Champagne bubbled and spilled all over my hand. All around me, people were passing around bottles and filling their glasses. Still no one spoke. Then Moira raised a brow to someone at the back, received some sort of confirmation, and gave a little nod.

'Good people,' she began, with surprising clarity. 'Today we celebrate the renaming of our town. We do this for a good reason. We are renaming the town to acknowledge the fact that we have changed... not so much economically, or industrially, or even socially... but rather that we have transcended to a new understanding of what it is to be a community. This is a significant achievement. I think that most of us here this morning can appreciate that, whilst nothing looks different, everything has changed—our lives are still the same, but we view ourselves completely differently. Very rarely, in the chronicle of human history, are communities able to achieve an accord that is relevant and lasting. When this occurs, it brings about a certain joy; we feel united and we feel part of something stronger; we feel immensely capable. We will meet the future with composure, because our values are simple and dear to our heart.

'You all know what precipitated this change in our town—a bizarre sequence of events that involved some brave and brilliant, naïve and foolish individuals, whose folly turned to fortune, and who enabled us to discover how good we can be—how fearless, how inspired, how considerate and tolerant.

'Now, I, for one, won't be giving up the technology that has made this possible, but the point is, we have arrived at a place that we have never been to before— ladies and gentlemen, I give you the township of Thrum!'

Well, we responded with a garbled, 'To the township of Thrum' and cheered and sculled copiously. There seemed to be an enormous supply of champagne at hand.

Moira waved her hand for quiet and, with the assistance of Max, maintained her place on the platform. The crowd hushed.

'Look, this is a secret that no one will believe—you know that, don't you. But, if anyone asks about the town's name, we'll just say that it has a good feel about it...'

I was gratified to hear, beneath the shrieks and cackles of the ladies, the hearty and uninhibited laughter of the menfolk who seemed to stand their ground and be happy for their women.

We didn't hang around; Moira had captured the moment and we all believed her. But our futures were individual, and the mention of a folly did rather compromise the prospect of a prolonged salutation to our town.

So, Sonya and I headed back and fell in with a long line of chattering townsfolk. My heart was beating faster than need be—I felt on the verge of something momentous, and yet I was being ignored in the most considerate way. People were pleasantly avoiding mention of my involvement with anything to do with the Glamorama. It was the only way, really—what could possibly be said to contribute to a harmless conversation that wasn't going to lead to awkwardness?

Sonya's arm was around me as we idled the last stretch to our corner. Then, I felt another arm encircle me. Tiffany grinned and dipped her eyes at me. 'Ian,' she said, 'why don't you tell our story. You pretty much know everyone's story... a bit of research here and there... it'd be...' and she trailed off and thought for a moment.

I turned to Sonya. She gave me that little smile that holds so much trust.

Tiffany continued, '... I don't know—it'd be a good story.'

Sonya gave me a squeeze. 'Why don't you—it is a good story, and it will keep you out of the shed. You get into so much trouble there.' We had a laugh, and bantered on until we got to the house.

We bade Tiffany cheerio and climbed up the stairs to the veranda.

A vision occupied my mind—a new incarnation for the shed—a desk with one of those new computers—a jug—a teapot—a tape recorder...

Sonya said, 'You can do up the old couch. That should be comfortable—but no gadgets.'

I walked to the corner of the high-set veranda that overlooks the shed and rested on the rail. I looked out across the rooftops, beyond Tiffany's house and panned over the road to Max and Phoebe's house. In the distance, I could see where the horizon is spiked by the thin chimneys and saw-toothed roofs of the abandoned abattoir after which the town was originally named.

A light breeze wafted the heat from the street onto my face. Something tickled at my hand and I looked down to see what it was. A passionfruit tendril, green and slender, reached out to me like the dendrite of an expanding consciousness.

I caressed the curling vine in my open hand.

THE END

Did you enjoy this book?

I'd love you to leave a review at
www.amazon.com.au/dp/1505392020/

Snap a pic of yourself and this book and post it on
Instagram using #petelansbooks

Please consider this book, or one of my other
books, as a gift for someone.

Find more of my books online at
www.amazon.com/Pete-Lans/e/B07D6FKB4Y/

If you would like to communicate with me
personally, please email
author@petelans.com

Free Short Story!

Email me at author@petelans.com for a FREE copy of
my short story, *Good Morning Sunshine*.

The Difference

- Twelve Journeys of Humor and Fulfilment -

The twelve short stories in this anthology illustrate how pathos shapes our experiences and that we are mostly unaware of the direction of our journey through life.

A harmless foray into the theatre leads to love... A man, mysteriously cursed, finds salvation in abject humiliation... Another, continually thwarted, discovers the legacy of all his ardour... A reckless young woman tests the boundaries of her privileged life... Can a man, a sportscar and a nymph exist in the same story?... Two cousins, worlds apart, discover that family comes first... ASIO and the Department of Education misplace their files and save the nation... An android reviews her journey amongst humans... A scurrilous landlord creates his own doom when he tries to save the world... Eternity is not something to look forward to... and, can a man redeem himself by not saying a thing?

Realm of the Conspirators

When a young, Australian stockman finds a mysterious briefcase at the site of a plane crash on his family's outback property, he and his girlfriend become ensnared in the labyrinth world of global conspirators.

Smuggled on board the world's fastest mega-yacht, they encounter assassins, drones and mind-rays as they visit exotic locations in their attempt to disarm the dominating elite's ultra-weapon before it annihilates the earth.

Warning—Reading this New Adult book might expose you to the attention of secret organizations and clandestine powers. This book contains ideas for some pretty wild technology and a whole lot of made-up stuff (well, it is fiction!) but no bad language.

www.ingramcontent.com/pod-product-compliance
Lightning Source LLC
Chambersburg PA
CBHW030647110726
47901CB00002B/596